THE WINDING ROAD

Judaic Traditions in Literature, Music, and Art
Ken Frieden, *Series Editor*

Select Titles in Judaic Traditions in Literature, Music, and Art

Diary of a Lonely Girl, or The Battle against Free Love
Miriam Karpilove; Jessica Kirzane, trans.

Once There Was Warsaw: A Memoir
Ber Kutsher; Gerald Marcus, trans.

The People of the Book and the Camera:
Photography in the Hebrew Novel
Ofra Amihay

"A Plague of Cholera" and Other Stories
Jonah Rosenfeld; Rachel Mines, trans.

"A Provincial Newspaper" and Other Stories
Miriam Karpilove; Jessica Kirzane, trans.

Questionable People: Inventing Modern Jewish
Selves in the Russian Empire, 1860–1890
Svetlana Natkovich

The Tears and Prayers of Fools: A Novel
Grigory Kanovich; Mary Ann Szporluk, trans.

War Lives: Revenge, Grief, and Conflict in Israeli Fiction
Nitza Ben-Dov

For a full list of titles in this series, visit:
https://press.syr.edu/supressbook-series
/judaic-traditions-in-literature-music-and-art/.

THE
WINDING
ROAD

My Childhood Years

Rokhl Feygenberg

Translated from the Yiddish by
Tamara T. Helfer

Syracuse University Press

This book was originally published in Yiddish as
Di kinder-yohren, in serial form in the monthly journal
Dos leben (Saint Petersburg, January–August 1905).

A Yiddish Book Center Translation
Copyright © 2026 by Syracuse University Press
Syracuse, New York 13244-5290

First Edition 2026

26 27 28 29 30 31   6 5 4 3 2 1

For a listing of books published and distributed by Syracuse University Press,
visit https://press.syr.edu.

ISBN: 9780815612063 (paperback)
9780815657699 (e-book)

Library of Congress Cataloging-in-Publication Data

Names: Feygenberg, Rakhel, 1885–1972 author |
Helfer, Tamara T. (Tamara Toby) translator
Title: The winding road : my childhood years / Rokhl Feygenberg ;
translated from the Yiddish by Tamara T. Helfer.
Other titles: Ḳinder-yohren. English
Description: First edition. | Syracuse, New York :
Syracuse University Press, 2026. | Series: Judaic traditions
in literature, music, and art | Includes bibliographical references.
Identifiers: LCCN 2025042723 (print) | LCCN 2025042724 (ebook) |
ISBN 9780815612063 paperback | ISBN 9780815657699 ebook
Subjects: LCSH: Feygenberg, Rakhel, 1885–1972—Childhood and youth—
Fiction | BISAC: FICTION / Jewish | FICTION / Cultural Heritage |
LCGFT: Autobiographical fiction | Novels | Fiction
Classification: LCC PJ5129.F43 K513 2026 (print) | LCC PJ5129.F43 (ebook)
LC record available at https://lccn.loc.gov/2025042723
LC ebook record available at https://lccn.loc.gov/2025042724

The authorized representative in the EU for product
safety and compliance is Mare Nostrum Group B.V.
Mauritskade 21D, 1091 GC Amsterdam, The Netherlands
gpsr@mare-nostrum.co.uk

Rokhl Feygenberg, age about twenty-five, ca. 1910. Courtesy of Daphna Levy. Photo digitally restored.

Contents

Translator's Introduction

In November 1904, the eminent essayist Zalman Epstein walked into the Saint Petersburg office of the Yiddish newspaper *Der fraynd* with a large parcel of some twenty-odd notebooks handwritten by a teenage girl from a tiny shtetl near Minsk.

The editor of *Der fraynd*, Shaul Ginzburg, was preparing for the inaugural edition of a new Yiddish literary magazine.[1] These were heady times for Ginzburg. Only two years earlier, the Russian authorities had unexpectedly granted permission for him to establish *Der fraynd*, the first Yiddish daily in czarist Russia.[2] Ginzburg had been determined to create a quality newspaper and had solicited literary material from the best Yiddish writers, including the three eminent *klasikers*, Mendele Moykher Sforim, Y. L. Peretz, and Sholem Aleichem; established novelists like Mordkhe Spektor and Yankev Dinezon; and younger writers like the poet Khayim-Nakhman Bialik and the novelist and playwright Sholem Asch. The success of *Der fraynd* had inspired Ginzburg and his staff to create a monthly supplement where they could publish longer literary works. The new magazine would be called *Dos leben* (*Life*), and its first issue was to be published in January 1905.

So when Epstein handed him the girl's notebooks, Ginzburg must have had his doubts. As he leafed through the notebooks, he saw that they were written without chapters or section breaks, and even without conventional punctuation—it would be no easy task to read. But Epstein told Ginzburg that this was a manuscript written by his niece, an orphan who was living with relatives in Odesa. Ginzburg knew Epstein as a courteous man with a fine, artistic taste, and he must have been moved when Epstein asked him to review the manuscript personally. "Don't take into account the fact that this is my niece," Epstein told him. "Just consider the impression that it makes on you."

When Ginzburg read the manuscript, he quickly grew captivated. The young author, Rokhl Feygenberg, had written about her own childhood shtetl, a tiny place tucked amidst forest and swampland and far from the cosmopolitan centers of the day. "There was an entire gallery of personalities, characters, and episodes," Ginzburg later wrote, "that felt true to life and very vivid." Feygenberg's style, he added, was simple but artistically sincere, and it was touching. Ginzburg's staff made some structural edits to break the story into chapters, inserted some necessary punctuation, and trimmed a few passages. No bigger revisions were needed, he recalled, and Rokhl Feygenberg's first publication, now named *Di kinder-yohren* (*My Childhood Years*), was serialized in eight monthly installments of *Dos leben* starting two months later, in the inaugural issue of January 1905.

This is the lightly fictionalized coming-of-age story of a woman who would go on to become one of the most celebrated Yiddish writers in eastern Europe.

Origins: Jews in the Russian Empire

Rokhl Feygenberg's birthplace of Lyuban, today a town in the country of Belarus, was typical for the shtetls that pervaded the western Russian Empire in the nineteenth century.

Western European Jews had first migrated eastward en masse in the wake of a series of expulsions centuries earlier and settled throughout what would become the Polish-Lithuanian Commonwealth in the mid sixteenth century. The Polish-Lithuanian Commonwealth covered an enormous geographic region that spanned from the Baltic Sea in the north (modern-day Poland, Lithuania, Latvia, and Estonia) down through modern-day Belarus and Ukraine all the way to the Black Sea in the south. The Commonwealth was unusual in its time in that it was a parliamentary government with an elected king; its localities were ruled by a powerful class of major and minor nobility and gentry, the *szlachta*, who held private ownership of its cities, towns, and villages as well as its vast rural estates.

The *szlachta* magnates encouraged immigration and settlement to its underpopulated and underdeveloped regions by those who could generate economic activity and therefore income from taxes. Jews were an ideal match to the needs of the *szlachta*: they could read and write and were skilled at carrying out commerce, even over long distances; furthermore, unlike other actual and would-be inhabitants of the multicultural Commonwealth—including gentile populations of Poles, Lithuanians, Germans, Belarusians, Ukrainians, and eastern Slavic peoples, among others—the Jews posed no threat to the ruling power of the *szlachta*. Poland became a haven for Jews all over Europe, and there was a period of nearly three hundred years of relative security for Jewish communities there. This is not to downplay the serious anti-Semitism, attacks, and pogroms that Jews faced throughout the Polish-Lithuanian Commonwealth in those centuries; nonetheless, these were relatively secure times, and Jews even enjoyed a certain amount of self-rule. The wandering people put down roots.

The political situation changed dramatically at the end of the eighteenth century, when the three surrounding expansionist powers of the Kingdom of Prussia, the Habsburg monarchy of Austria, and the Russian Empire took advantage of the weakened leadership of the Polish-Lithuanian Commonwealth and seized and divided among themselves the extensive Commonwealth lands in a series of three "Partitions." Russia gained nearly two-thirds of the former

Commonwealth territory, and about a million Jews who lived in this vast area suddenly became inhabitants of the Russian Empire. This was a novel situation for Russia, which had earlier forbidden Jews from even entering their country; now suddenly they had inherited the largest population of Jews in the world.

The political, administrative, and social upheavals that resulted in the Jewish community of the Russian Empire continued throughout the nineteenth century as different rulers tried various approaches to managing their recently acquired Jewish subjects, who generally remained confined to the lands of the former Commonwealth that later came to be known as the "Pale of Settlement." After a couple of decades of relative calm following the Partitions, the situation changed quickly after 1825 under the rule of the reactionary and repressive tsar Nicholas I, nicknamed "Haman the Second" by the Jews after the cruel villain in the biblical Book of Esther. Over the course of his thirty-year rule, Nicholas I enacted hundreds of anti-Jewish laws; perhaps the most notorious of these resulted in the forced conscription of Jewish boys as young as eight for twenty-five-year duties of service in the Russian army.

The next tsar, Alexander II, who ruled 1855–81, ended many of the harshest policies of his predecessor but instead implemented policies meant to encourage Jews to assimilate. Under his reign, for example, Jews who completed secondary education in Russian (rather than Jewish) schools were allowed greater rights, such as the right of residence in Russia proper, outside the Pale. But after Alexander II was assassinated in 1881, the situation for Jews once again turned precarious, with hundreds of anti-Jewish pogroms carried out over the following two years and the enactment of the repressive "May Laws" in 1882, which severely limited land ownership and the leasing of property to Jews, including the inns and taverns like the ones Feygenberg's maternal family had apparently run for generations, and which forbade Jews from living in rural areas. Feygenberg refers to this period obliquely in chapter 1 of the present work, when her aunts and their families had to uproot their lives in response: "None of them wanted to leave the villages where they had lived for such a long time, and they wept as they bade farewell to every little tree and blade of grass." In subsequent years, laws were enacted to severely limit the number of Jews allowed to study at Russian schools and universities, and nearly all Jews were expelled from Moscow.

It was in the midst of this tumultuous period that Rokhl Feygenberg was born in her little shtetl of Lyuban in 1885.

Lyuban and Its Environment

Lyuban, fictionalized vividly as "Bulin" in *My Childhood Years*, was a small, isolated place during Feygenberg's childhood. Within the Pale of Settlement, Lyuban was situated within the region known as

White Russia (modern Belarus) in the Minsk "gubernia," an administrative unit similar in scale to an American state, which itself was divided into nine districts, or counties. Lyuban lay in the district of Bobruisk about one hundred kilometers from the city of the same name, fictionalized as "Rabinsk." At the end of the nineteenth century, the nearest railroad was still far away in Bobruisk,[3] and the nearest small city of Slutsk, fictionalized as "Seltz," with its 14,000 residents,[4] was no easy trip, of fifty kilometers over poor roads. Geographically, Lyuban and its environs lay at the edge of vast forests and swampland, and the roads, shtetls, and villages were mired in mud for three-quarters of the year.[5] With casual travel so difficult, the residents were at the mercy of their coachmen for trade, post, and contact with the outside world.

The Lyuban of Feygenberg's childhood was a classic shtetl, a Jewish market town. The Russian census of 1897, the year Feygenberg was twelve years old and her mother began to be seriously ill, listed 774 residents in Lyuban, and fully 95 percent of them were Jews.[6] Lyuban had three synagogues, a rabbi, a ritual slaughterer, and a bath house. The shtetl was known for its fine carpentry and chairs, which were sold in Bobruisk, and for its ducks, which were fattened for the same market.[7] It was not uncommon for the young women of Lyuban to work for a few years as domestics in the homes of wealthy Jewish families in Bobruisk to earn enough money to bring a dowry back to the shtetl. There were also artisans and

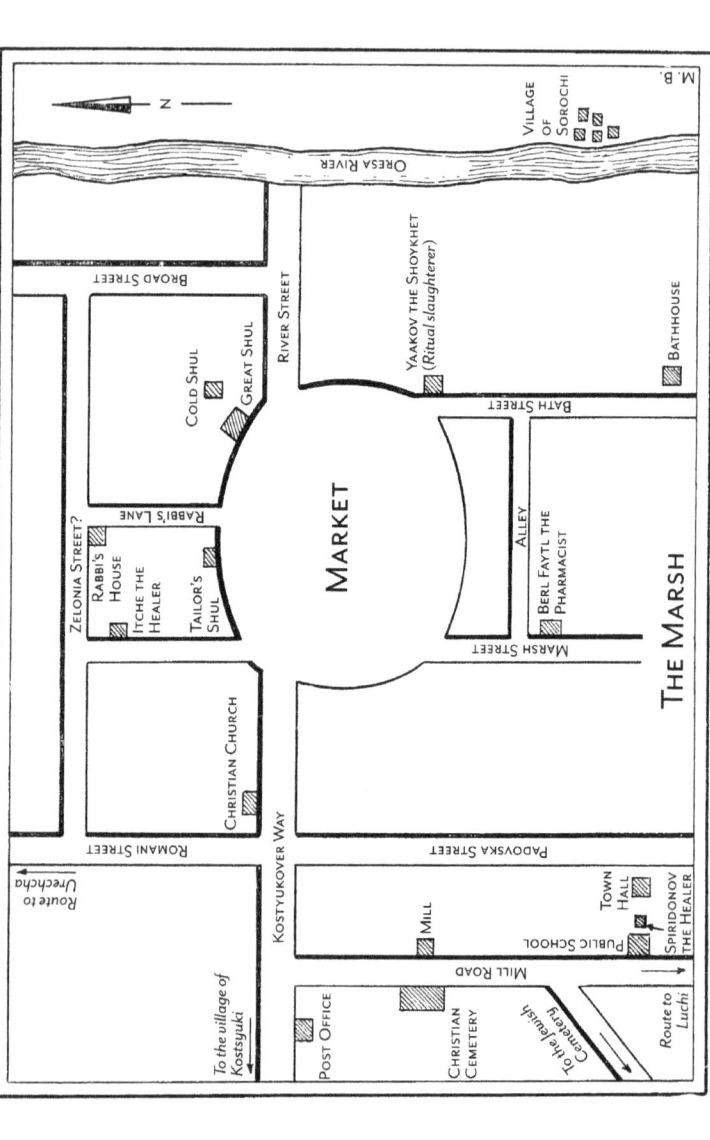

Opposite page: Map of Lyuban, Belarus, drawn by an unknown person with initials M. B., undated but probably drawn from memory ca. 1950–62 to represent Lyuban in a period earlier in the twentieth century. Feygenberg described living close to the Cold Shul and said that the front section of their house, with the family's general store, faced the "main street." In chapter 3, Oreh the melamed lived "way over on Romani Street," and the village of Sorochi is fictionalized as "Kalatsia" in chapter 5. The Jewish cemetery was built sometime after the death of Feygenberg's father (ca. 1889) and before that of her mother (ca. 1900). Reprinted from *Slutsk and Vicinity Memorial Book* (1962), 217, courtesy of Dorot Jewish Division, the New York Public Library. New York Public Library Digital Collections. https://digitalcollections .nypl.org/items/f6dfc840-74eb-0133-bf27-00505686d14e (accessed January 28, 2025). The original labels were written in Yiddish and Hebrew; English labels were added by Patrick Remer and Zinnia Heinzmann.

craftsmen who made candles, and pipes for smoking, and like other nearby shtetls, there would have been tailors, butchers, carpenters, bricklayers, and peddlers. But the majority of Jews in Lyuban, as in other shtetls in the area, were likely shopkeepers.

Feygenberg's maternal grandmother Feyga-Beyla Shapira left Lyuban in about 1876[8] with four of her five children (sons Zalman and Yitzhak and daughters Khaya and Nekhama[9]) to join Feygenberg's grandfather, Nakhum Epstein, in Odesa. When they left Lyuban, the grandparents entrusted their home to their newly married daughter Sarah and her husband, the widower and rabbinical scholar Ber Feygenberg—Feygenberg's parents. The house was beautiful and spacious, with courtyard buildings and a large plot for growing vegetables that provided food for the family throughout the year. Nonetheless, cash was a problem for the couple. Ber had spent his entire dowry on books, and tiny Lyuban did not produce enough students to let him earn a living as a tutor to support his young family along with his teenage son from his first marriage. Instead, the couple lived apart, with Ber moving to Bobruisk to be a tutor, and Sarah earning her own small income from sewing fine household linens, which were particularly valued by the Russian Orthodox priest's wife and daughters. As in *My Childhood Years*, Sarah and Ber fought, including over Ber's son, but as Feygenberg later recalled, whenever her father came home to Lyuban, "their house filled with light, and my mother's face would brighten"—and the shtetl's most esteemed residents would gather to hear the rabbinical scholar's intellectual discourse.

After Ber's untimely death when Rokhl was about four, his twenty-nine-year-old widow resisted her family's suggestion to join them in Odesa. Instead, she traveled to Slutsk, sold her husband's extensive library to a wealthy merchant there, and used the proceeds to open her own general store in the front section of her home, which she had previously rented out for income. The storefront faced the main street, and Sarah had a head for business; the shop quickly became popular with Jews and gentiles alike and even did well enough for her to establish a charitable lending fund for the shtetl's peddlers.

Life in Lyuban during the week would generally have been quiet and dominated by the rhythm of Jewish social and religious customs. But on Sundays, the gentiles who lived in the rural areas and nearby villages would have poured in to the shtetl to go to church, sell their products (cheese, butter, wood, poultry, calves, dried pelts, etc.), buy their weekly goods from the shtetl's shopkeepers, and perhaps spend any extra money at the tavern. A resident of the nearby shtetl of Hlusk later recalled that on Sundays, when their trading was finished, the gentiles would often get drunk and "make a little pogrom" in the market place, forcing the shopkeepers to close their stores until the shtetl's butchers and horse traders showed up to quiet the drunkards.[10] This helps to explain the lament of Feygenberg's young narrator in chapter 8 when she says, "But oh, how I hated Sunday, with all of its drunk gentiles!"

Feygenberg's Early Education

There was no school for girls in the Lyuban of Feygenberg's youth. As Feygenberg later recalled, she studied Yiddish, Russian, and a bit of arithmetic with a Jew who was called "the teacher," and she studied Tanakh in the evenings with their neighbor, Reb Yedidya the melamed.[11] Later, she and two other girls from wealthy families were tutored together and learned to read and write Hebrew using an ancient method: they read chapters from the Torah while their tutor translated word by word into Yiddish.[12] The shtetl's very young boys would have learned by a similar method, but as a class, in cheder.

As with her narrator, Feygenberg's education came to an abrupt halt when she was twelve, circa 1897, when she took over running the household as well as the family store after her mother became seriously ill.[13] In her spare time, she read voraciously— both the traditional tales and moralistic readings for women from her grandmother the rebbetzin's library, as well as the popular romance novels of the day. She was enthralled by the prolific novelist Shomer, the pen name of Nakhum Meyer Shaykevitsh, whose books were wildly popular but not considered quality literary material.[14]

Feygenberg was not only reading at this young age, but she was also already writing, especially when she had free time in the store. In chapter 4 of this work, she has her narrator writing creative letters for the residents of the shtetl at the age of about twelve, a memory Feygenberg developed decades later into a short story called "My First Readers." At thirteen, obsessed with the romance novels she was reading, Feygenberg wrote her own called *Yosef and Rosa*, which caused such an uproar in her home that she had to burn the manuscript.[15] These are also the names of the ill-fated protagonist lovers from *The Dark Young Man* by Yankev Dinezon, a book that is mentioned in chapter 8 of the present work and that was the first

Yiddish bestseller. Feygenberg's narrator says she retold the story several times to the girls in the shtetl,
and "it felt like I had written it myself." Feygenberg
may well have done so in her own version of *Yosef
and Rosa*.

The Odesa Years

In about 1900, about a year after the death of her
mother, her grandmother brought Feygenberg from
Lyuban to Odesa, a journey that would have brought
them first by coach to Bobruisk or Minsk, where they
would have caught a series of crisscrossing trains
down to the famous city on the Black Sea.[16]

Odesa features in *My Childhood Years* as the ro-
manticized "Rishelev,"[17] the cosmopolitan city in the
south of the Russian Pale where Feygenberg's maternal grandfather Nakhum Epstein settled as a tutor
after his failed attempts as a builder of mills, and
where her grandmother, uncles, and aunts had moved
to join him nearly ten years before Feygenberg was
born.

Odesa in 1900 was huge by any standard that
Feygenberg could have imagined. It was modern,
cosmopolitan, and new, having been established as
a city only one hundred years previously. Until 1859,
it had enjoyed special status as a free port, which
had attracted a diverse population of traders, and by
the turn of the twentieth century, Odesa was a multicultural city with 400,000 residents, over a third
of whom were Jews from all over Europe.[18] It was

a beautiful place, with fine boulevards and parks, splendid theaters, and a boardwalk extending past the port where residents could stroll and look out on the expanse of the Black Sea.

But modernization and industrialization had also led to sweatshops, slums, and dark little apartments, and Odesa was flush with haves and have-nots, roiling politics, religious tension, and social unrest. All over the Russian Empire, Jewish communities were still reeling from the repressive May Laws and the pogroms that continued, and Jews were leaving; more than two million Jews would emigrate from Russia before 1920, many heading to the United States and to Palestine. Odesa had become an important center of political activism for Jews, especially for Zionism, but a significant economic downturn combined with onerous conditions for workers also drove an active socialist movement in the form of the Jewish Labor Bund. Culturally there were additional tensions in the Jewish community between the old ways and the new, between traditionalism and modernism, between orthodoxy and secularism, and between young and old. This was the Odesa that Rokhl Feygenberg encountered when she arrived from her little shtetl of Lyuban at the age of about fifteen.

When Feygenberg arrived in Odesa, she moved in with her grandmother and spent her first year acclimating to her new life and studying Russian with a tutor.[19] Despite her years of yearning to live in a big city, she found she had a hard time adjusting. She felt strange and lost, and she studied the cheerful schoolgirls she saw in the streets, and their colorful uniforms, with as much irritation as fascination.[20] After the stressful years of her mother's illness and death and the upheaval of her transition to Odesa, she soon had a new concern: word had come that her little brother Yitzhak, who had always been sickly, was seriously ill. As in *My Childhood Years*, Yitzhak had gone off to the Mir Yeshiva when Rokhl moved to Odesa, but unlike in the story, Feygenberg later recalled that he was pleased to go and spent a happy six months studying there. Now, however, he had suddenly fallen ill, and he abandoned the yeshiva and moved back home to Lyuban. In Odesa, it may have already been clear from the reports she received that her last remaining family member, her closest companion from her youngest age through the years of their mother's decline, was dying.

She walked through the streets of Odesa then, reliving the painful scenes from her childhood and filled with suffering. She remembered her mother, struggling to breathe, and she imagined Yitzhak pale and dying in Lyuban, while she lacked for nothing in her new home. And then, on a fortuitous day she described decades later, her tutor arrived with a collection of Russian stories for language study; among them was a story written by a girl about her childhood, describing how she helped her father with his farm work in the village. "This discovery thrilled me," Feygenberg recalled, "as if I had stumbled across something precious. At once, I realized—I, too, could write about myself."

She bought a notebook that very day and began writing feverishly, day and night, "pouring all my sorrow into the writing until I finished the tale." Her description complements her publisher Shaul Ginzburg's recollection of the twenty-odd notebooks that comprised *My Childhood Years*, which he described as written "as if poured from one casting."[21]

Feygenberg's writing of *My Childhood Years* was intensely personal. Whether stung by the memory of her earlier writing of *Yosef and Rosa* back in the shtetl, or leery of her conservative grandmother's reaction, or simply trying to handle her strong feelings privately, she kept it secret and the manuscript hidden while living with her grandmother. Decades later, Feygenberg also explained why it was the only one of her books she never translated into Hebrew: "I lacked the emotional strength to relive the suffering I had endured in my childhood, [which] remained infused in my blood my entire life."[22]

After she achieved a level of mastery in Russian, Feygenberg's family wanted her to pursue some kind of intellectual endeavor, in alignment with the family tradition. Her uncles, who took charge of her education, were prominent Zionists who had themselves come of age in Odesa after their arrival from Lyuban as teenagers in 1876. As a young man, Zalman Epstein[23] had wanted to go to university but was refused admission as a Jew. While he earned his living as a bookkeeper and from commerce, he began publishing his writings in 1879 and was well established as an essayist and a Zionist activist by the turn of the century, serving for ten years as the secretary of the board of the Society of Lovers of Zion in Odesa. In 1904—significantly for Feygenberg—he would move to Saint Petersburg and become an editor for the short-lived Yiddish daily, *Der tog*. His younger brother Yitzhak Epstein[24] had moved to Rosh Pina, one of the first Zionist settlements in what was then Ottoman-ruled Palestine, back in 1886, and he became prominent as an educator and linguist, making contributions to transform the written biblical language of Hebrew into a modern spoken tongue. In 1903, when he was nearly forty years old, Yitzhak traveled to Lausanne, Switzerland, to complete the university studies that had also been denied him as a young man, and he later earned a doctorate there.

Feygenberg bucked the intellectual leanings of her family and instead took up the proletarian occupation of sewing. Despite her grandmother's dismay at this pursuit of manual labor,[25] she got a job working in a high-end women's salon. Her work as a seamstress put her in close proximity to Odesa's sweatshop workers and helped to reinforce lifelong socialist sympathies.

Feygenberg's life was about to take another dramatic turn. Some time after her grandmother immigrated to Palestine and Feygenberg moved in with her Aunt Nekhama in Odesa, her aunt discovered her notebooks.[26] By early 1904, Feygenberg was about eighteen and had probably been working as a seamstress for two or three years. When her aunt found the manuscript, Feygenberg was mortified and begged her not to show it to her uncle Zalman Epstein, who was coming to visit for Passover from his new job in Saint Petersburg. It is hard to be certain of the source of her embarrassment: was it because it was so private, or because she was nervous about the prospect of showing her girlish writing to her renowned essayist uncle, or because she had an eighteen-year-old's natural embarrassment toward her own fifteen-year-old self? In any case, Aunt Nekhama did give Uncle Zalman the manuscript, and Uncle Zalman read it, and afterward, he came to young Rokhl with a kiss. Even if this effort was a one-time occurrence, he said, the book was good; it had been written by a true writer. With this proclamation, Zalman Epstein brought Feygenberg's manuscript back to Saint Petersburg and gave it to Shaul Ginzburg.

In the few short biographies of Rokhl Feygenberg, the story is repeated that Feygenberg got her start as a writer when her uncle Zalman Epstein brought the manuscript of *My Childhood Years* to Shaul Ginzburg, and Ginzburg published her work. But from Feygenberg's own recollection, as recounted above, it is clear that there were two overlooked women who were critically important to her development as a writer: first, a Russian girl, anonymous to us, who wrote a story about herself,[27] and second, her aunt Nekhama, who found Feygenberg's manuscript and recognized it as being worthy of handing over to her writer brother.

Here is the story that captivated its early readers and launched Rokhl Feygenberg's seven-decade writing career.

Translation Notes

The Winding Road: My Childhood Years is Rokhl Feygenberg's (1885–1972) lightly fictionalized coming-of-age story, originally published as *Di kinder-yohren*, or *My Childhood Years*. This translation is based on the serialized version of the novel, written by the teenage Feygenberg and published in eight installments of the monthly journal *Dos leben* in 1905. Feygenberg later reworked the story somewhat and published it in book form in 1909 by HaShakar Press in Warsaw.

As described in the Introduction, the original manuscript was written as one long narrative, without chapter breaks. I preserved the chapter breaks as inserted by the editors of *Dos leben* and took the liberty of adding titles to the chapters, and I added section breaks within chapters as well. The 1909 book version of *My Childhood Years* does not have chapters and has very few section breaks.

To aid the modern reader, I occasionally added language as a gloss to elucidate terms or concepts that would have been familiar to Feygenberg's contemporary audience. In some passages, I edited the text lightly or rearranged sentences for clarity. To guide the reader through the somewhat confusing genealogy originally presented without names in the first chapter, I added the names of Feygenberg's own relatives. In the original, some characters were given names in later chapters but not when the characters were first introduced, and on occasion, a named character was given a different name in later installments of the serialization; for clarity, I inserted the names of characters when they first appeared and chose one name for each character.

The two original prologues to the 1905 and 1909 versions of the book are completely different from one another, and both are confusing and stylistically incongruent with the straightforward presentation of the rest of the story. It seems likely that neither was written contemporaneously with the rest of the narrative. Instead, I rewrote a brief prologue, using Feygenberg's own words but in a condensed, direct tone that aligns with the style of the book. I also used parts of her two original prologues in conjunction with an excerpt of Feygenberg's contribution[1] to the 1962 *Slutsk and Vicinity Memorial Book* to create a brief epilogue that was not at all part of the original story, again using her own words. My new epilogue includes the story of her brother Yitzhak's death, which was referred to obliquely in the opening to chapter 2 but otherwise not included in the original text of *My Childhood Years*. As detailed in the Introduction, it appears that Feygenberg may have written the majority of *My Childhood Years* when Yitzhak was dying but still alive, which could explain why his death is otherwise omitted from the narrative.

The 1909 book form is broadly similar to the 1905 serialized version, but a few sections contain important differences; Judith Levin gives a detailed accounting of these differences in her 2022 thesis.[2] In general, the changes act to soften some of the more negative depictions of shtetl life; for example, the 1909 version omits the existence of the narrator's baby brother Nakhumke entirely and thereby avoids the depiction of his tragic death. Where the 1905 and 1909 versions diverge, I found the earlier version to be more unfiltered and truer to the perspective of a fifteen-year-old girl, which is why I chose to translate the original work.

There are many small choices a translator must wrestle with. For example, Feygenberg presents her narrator's birth shtetl as in "Lithuania," by which she meant both a literal geographical region covering modern Lithuania, Belarus, and Latvia, as well as a specific subculture of eastern European Jewry. My choice was to render this as "White Russia," which is the historical term for Belarus, where her shtetl was located, but which does not connote the intended cultural nuance. In chapter 4, for example, Feygenberg's narrator describes the cold parenting style of mothers that is traditional in White Russia (again my rendering of her "Lithuania"), which is consonant with the stereotypical stoic, intellectual nature of her subculture.

My choices of spelling and transliteration of names and Yiddish words are my own. They are usually based on the YIVO standardization of Yiddish orthography, except where I thought the pronunciation might lead to confusion for an English-reading audience; for example, I use *Shabbes* instead of the standardized *Shabes* to denote the Jewish sabbath. Names like Yente and Malke that end with an "e" are pronounced as "Yen-teh" and "Mal-keh." It was particularly difficult to choose how to present the author's name; her first name has been represented as Rokhl, Rokhel, Rakhel, Rachel, and Rachela, and her surname as Faygnberg, Faygenberg, Feygenberg, Faigenberg, and Fajgenberg. All of these are acceptable presentations of what I have chosen to render as Rokhl Feygenberg. However spelled, the pronunciation of the first syllable of her surname rhymes with the English word "eye."

The novel is set in a small Belarusian shtetl at the end of the nineteenth century.

THE WINDING ROAD

Prologue

Not long ago, I visited my birthplace, a small shtetl in White Russia, for the first time since I was a child. Now that I live in a beautiful city in the south of Russia, it may seem as if I am used to my modern life, where everything is nicer than in my muddy little shtetl, but my former home is always on my mind. My childhood years there were not good ones, but I long for them nonetheless.

The shtetl where I was born lies in a secluded corner of the vast swamplands of Polesia, amidst razed forests and huge marshes, dense with grass. If I could grow wings and soar high above the earth, I would see a broad, flat land, hundreds of miles long and lush with dreamy green forests, a land with long, flowing streams set in eroded banks, and storm-tossed lakes with tall hills by their sides. A white stone highway stretches out over the land, and far away, at the edge of the sky, a winding, muddy road leaves the noisy highway, wanders past lonesome forests with sad, thin trees, past the stumps of giant oaks, and comes to meet my shtetl.

As I approached my former home through the forest over that winding, muddy road, it looked like a paradise to me: splayed out on God's earth with ease, surrounded by green gardens and golden fields with haystacks, embellished with a low, smoky woodland on one side and a rippling stream on the other. The river stretched past the shtetl in an arc, wrapped around it like a blue embroidered ribbon, and lost itself somewhere far away in the forest.

The shtetl comprised only three small roads and a couple of hundred little cottages. There was our shul with its leaky roof, and the white church in the middle of the market with its great, tall windows, and next to the priest's garden, there was the well with its clear, healthy water. There were no large buildings.

We were protected by God himself. He had covered all our roads, the Jewish as well as the Christian, with one sky, like a ceiling laid with stone. The sky shielded our old shul with its weeping gray walls, and it shielded the church with the neglected cross on its spire. The wind passed through freely, and the people did too. Here, there was a place for everyone.

My soul grew in this very land. This is where I was born and where I spent my childhood years. Let the angry winds chase me to the corners of the world, but my home will remain forever here. I will carry it in my heart, like a hidden treasure, and when I yearn for my home, I will sketch its portrait on these pages with my tears.

1

Origins

I was born in White Russia in the small shtetl of Bulin, where both sides of my family played prominent roles. My paternal grandfather, Yaakov, was a rabbi in the shtetl, and my maternal grandfather, Nakhum, was its most respected homeowner and a gabbai, a top official in the synagogue.

My great-grandfather, Nakhum's father, had been the shtetl's richest homeowner. He too was a gabbai in the same shul, and he managed the shtetl's tavern as well. In those days, the Polish landowners still controlled the leases on the taverns in our part of White Russia. My great-grandfather was able to speak Polish, and he used to travel to pay his rent to the local nobleman, who treated him as a welcome visitor. Back then, every Polish landowner would typically have "his" Jew, who stood higher in his eyes than the others, and my great-grandfather was one of these lucky ones. As a consequence, his children also occupied the highest ranks, both in community matters as well as in business affairs. Briefly put, the entire family was among the elite, not only in the shtetl, but in the whole surrounding region.

My great-grandfather had eight daughters and one son. For every daughter whom he married off, he gave a dowry of a tavern in a nearby village by securing the lease from the local nobleman; he wanted his children and their descendants to be provided for throughout their lives. It seems that my great-grandfather was, as one would say, a very clever man, but he simply could not have understood that for Jews, there is no such thing as this kind of security. He could not have known that several decades later, in the years just before I was born, the laws would change and Jews would be prohibited from leasing taverns, and his children would be forced to leave their village inns to seek their fortune elsewhere.

By my time, some of those children, my great-aunts and their families, had already left for America. None of them wanted to leave the villages where they had lived for such a long time, and they wept as they bade farewell to every little tree and blade of grass. The majority chose to stay, however, despite the hardships they were facing. Whatever happens, they thought to themselves, we won't die of hunger; we'll find a way to live, so we won't have to carry ourselves off to the other side of the ocean. This is how most of my great-grandfather's children came to stay in their beloved homeland until the present day. By now a lot of them have died, but at least they are in our cemetery, with family; they weren't forced to lie among strangers.

Nowadays, my relatives are not as attached to their homeland as their parents had been. Every year they leave in droves, and they have scattered throughout the world. They go wherever their feet can carry them, to try to escape the problems here at home. And in the end, when they finally make it to some new place, the first thing they do is they write to say there is nothing good there either!

What I've described so far is about my great-grandfather's eight daughters, who had to leave their father's home to go with their husbands, even to the end of the world. But the foundation of a family is its sons, of course, and especially an only son like my grandfather Nakhum. It simply never would have occurred to my great-grandfather that Nakhum would not live out his years where his forefathers had lived before him. Nakhum's own grandfather had lived his entire life in our shtetl and died at the ripe old age of seventy-five, surrounded by his children, his grandchildren, and his great-grandchildren, who together numbered more than seventy souls. This was even more than the patriarch Jacob had when he entered Egypt! In the blessings which my great-grandfather gave to Nakhum before he died, I suspect he recited the prayer that his son should not become a homeless wanderer. Or perhaps this never occurred to him, because how could it possibly be otherwise? Such thoughts never entered his head. But I believe this from the following story, which my grandmother told me long ago, and which she learned from her mother-in-law, Nakhum's mother.

One day, when my grandfather was a little boy, a Romani woman came to their tavern. When she saw how his parents doted on young Nakhum, she prophesized to his mother that her only son would not remain at home. The Romani said that when Nakhum grew up, he would travel far away and rarely return; he would even die in a distant land, and his children would also live far away. When my great-grandmother told this story, she said, "Only a Romani would say these kinds of things, damn her!" She knew that it was normal for a Romani to roam from one corner of the world to the other without having any fixed home. But this kind of wandering was unthinkable for Jewish homeowners like them, and rich ones at that—they expected to grow old in the same place they were born and raised. They were settled; Nakhum's father held the tavern lease and had the honor of being the gabbai in the synagogue and the kosher meat tax collector, and they had seats with all the prominent people along the eastern wall of the synagogue. Even when they raised their children and married them off, the children remained nearby. They did not wander. And besides that, young Nakhum was such a great little fellow, such a fine scholar, and such a master of the holy language that the rabbi wished that he himself would be so blessed. So how could that Romani barge in from God knows where and say that he would grow up to live far away in a distant land and even die there?

Nakhum's father had never gone anywhere except the city of Rabinsk, thirteen miles from our shtetl. Why should he travel; did he not have a livelihood at home? His plan was to make a match for his son and to hand over a room in the tavern to him and his new wife. His daughter-in-law would have babies, and Nakhum's parents would run the tavern and help her raise the little ones so that Nakhum could sit and study Talmud until he was thirty years old. And when they themselves got to be old, my great-grandparents would move in to the room in the tavern and retire, and Nakhum and his wife would carry on the business. Before then, their son would have many years to complete his studies.

This was how Nakhum's father had plotted out his future, disregarding the foolish Romani, that vagabond, who'd had the audacity to say that a child from such a respectable home would end up wandering about among strangers. Their son didn't even go away to study at a yeshiva since they didn't want to let him leave the shtetl; instead, they paid the rabbi a lot of money for Nakhum to study with him there at home.

My great-grandparents cherished their little boy. I know this not only because of the story about the Romani's prophesying, but also from the following fact. When my great-grandmother was pregnant with him, she vowed that if she had a boy, she would donate wine to the shul for Shabbes as long as she lived. Her vow was so important to the family that sixty years later, with my grandfather already dead these eight years, I myself still make sure to donate wine to my shul every week. And when I visited my shtetl, the Shabbes wine was still donated to the shul by the remaining members of our family. From all this, I understand how his parents doted on my grandfather and trembled at the thought of letting him out of their sight. But Nature and her caprices do not ask for anyone's advice; my grandfather would indeed spend much of his adult life wandering, despite his parents' plans.

My grandfather Nakhum was endowed with extraordinary intelligence. Even as a child, instead of going off to play when he didn't have to study, he preferred to seclude himself in the garret, where he used to build little mills and all kinds of mechanical apparatuses. This hobby meant the world to him. He had to keep it a secret, however, because what was he, some kind of common carpenter's son, that he occupied himself with such things? But no matter how he tried to hide his tinkering, he would invariably get caught, and he would promise not to spend his time on such things anymore. He would always forget his promise, though, and return to his mechanics.

One time he presented his mother with a gift: he had built a pepper mill. His parents were very pleased with it. After this, as a reward for the pepper mill, he no longer had to hide himself in the garret, but he could carve and tap away in the tavern in plain sight. His parents were still not pleased with his work; but nonetheless, because they doted on him, they gave in and kept silent.

My grandfather's childhood passed quickly; he was married off at eighteen. His parents arranged a match for him from the big city, from Rabinsk. My grandfather did not see his bride before the wedding but relied on his father's expert judgment, and it turned out that my great-grandfather was indeed a maven: my grandmother Feyga was a very pretty brunette.

My grandmother Feyga was an orphan and was raised by her grandparents in the city of Rabinsk. Because she was an orphan, no one hurried to make a match for her, and she remained a spinster until she was twenty. Even though she was very pretty, her small-town sisters-in-law thought she was nothing in comparison with their brother Nakhum. They did not appreciate her beautiful black eyes, her pretty eyelashes, her long dark hair, or her two cheeks that bloomed like roses. They didn't notice any of this; they only saw that she was dark complexioned. A white face, it turns out, was valued more in those days than shining black eyes. I don't believe my grandmother ever knew that she had beautiful eyes. I'm certain no one ever told her this, and she had little time to look at herself in the mirror.

My grandmother apparently had an unhappy childhood, even though her grandfather, Reb Israel, was an enlightened Maskil who was a doctor as well as a great scholar. Reb Israel was a good, pious man. He and another man named Kushelevski, who later played a big role in the medical world, were the first Jewish doctors to come out of the Vilna Academy. Kushelevski became more famous than Reb Israel because he got his medical diploma and Reb Israel did not, even though both finished at the same time. Reb Israel did not get his diploma because he did not want to part with his beard and *peyes*, his sidelocks. This did not prevent him from having the largest practice in Rabinsk, however, since he was a good doctor and a congenial person. More than anything, he was valued for his kindness.

His wife was completely different and had a hateful character. She made the servants suffer, and my grandmother Feyga got her share too. As an orphan living with a difficult grandmother, Feyga was always kept busy. When she did have a bit of free time, she devoted it to an important matter: learning how to pray. Her grandmother had hired a melamed to teach her for one term, but Feyga couldn't master everything in such a short period. So because she wanted to know how to pray, she studied by herself. She was very devout, and she wanted to pray properly, like other pious women. She constantly applied herself, and she practiced all the time. This is how she got into the habit of praying every day, even though she made mistakes, and she prayed like this her entire life, with the same mistakes. This didn't bother her, because she had read in some prayer book that using proper Hebrew was less important than having good intentions. My grandmother could pride herself on that; she prayed with her entire heart, even with mistakes.

My grandmother had a lot of religious books. She loved *tkhines*, the women's prayers, which were easier to read since they were written in Yiddish instead of Hebrew, as well as books of moral instruction. She collected a large library of old prayer books, which did not gather dust in her home; she read them all the time and knew them very well. But the one thing that really bothered her was that she could not write. She complained whenever she had to ask her children to compose letters for her, since she did not like to ask them for favors. She laid the blame for not being able to write on her grandmother.

My grandmother was so pious that she took on all her tasks with love. She did also appropriate a bit of her grandmother's character, from which I subsequently suffered a lot. Nonetheless my grandmother was a dear. She was truly devout and very charitable, though she gave to charity not because she had compassion for the poor, but because she wanted the mitzvah for doing so. In her view, she was giving an advance to God, and she was completely confident that God would pay her back, with interest. But however egoistic my grandmother was with her charity and her assistance, she really did worry about others more than herself. She was highly esteemed by everyone.

When my grandmother Feyga arrived in our little shtetl from the big city of Rabinsk, from the aristocratic house of Reb Israel the doctor, she was not met with luxury in her new home. She arrived at her father-in-law's old tavern and was given a large bedroom. There were holes in the walls of the room that were so large that cats slipped in from outdoors, but that was only in summer. In winter the snow blew in through the holes. So much snow blew in one time that my grandmother's feather comforter turned white overnight. But my grandmother was not cold, because in those days people used two comforters, both of them thick, not at all like today, thank God—these days, you get a comforter, and there's only a handful of feathers inside. My grandmother wasn't afraid of sleeping in her cold room when she was under her comforters. She didn't complain, and she was completely satisfied with her new life, even though the customs there were cruder than at her grandfather's. One cannot forget that, in spite of everything, her in-laws were powerful people, and she was their only daughter-in-law. Furthermore, she was influenced by her husband Nakhum himself. She had never seen him before their wedding; no one had asked for her opinion about the match, just as they hadn't asked her groom. They simply congratulated her and said that she was lucky to be a bride. What my grandmother thought and dreamed about her bridegroom before the wedding, I won't attempt to describe, but afterward, she really loved him. Perhaps this was because a wife was supposed to love her husband. My grandmother lived her life this way for many happy years.

My grandmother Feyga had three daughters and two sons, and, unlike most small-shtetl mothers, she gave them all an education. She gave the boys to the best melamdim. They learned well, since they were very smart, and my grandmother rewarded their progress with white bread. Everyone predicted that they would grow up to be the greatest rabbis; my grandmother certainly hoped for a golden chair in paradise. But God had other designs for them.

With her daughters, my grandmother also had no reason to complain: they were pretty, smart, and talented. But my grandmother thought this was superfluous. Why should a girl be all this? Would this help her make a soup? As my grandmother used to say, what was meant for the girls, should be spent on the boys. But however poor my grandmother's opinions were of women's rights, she did send her eldest daughter Sarah away to the city for three months so she could learn how to write. A girl should at least know how to write a letter, she said, so if she should marry someone from another city or shtetl, she could write home. As soon as her daughter had finished the course, my grandmother bought some nice half-linen fabric and sat her down to sew some blouses and a trousseau. Her daughter was an excellent seamstress, and she was worthy of the best clothes that could be sewn, such as no other girl in our shtetl had ever seen. Truth be told, Sarah really was the greatest of all the girls, on the basis of her lineage as well as by virtue of her beauty, talent, and education; my grandmother was not deluded about her value. She knew very well that she had a gifted daughter, and she wanted to make good use of her: she intended to attract a rabbi as a son-in-law. And why not? Her pedigree was suitable, and it should be said, their fortune was as well.

Although there was not sufficient commerce in our shtetl to permit my grandmother Feyga to save enough for a dowry to attract a rabbi for a son-in-law, God had given them the necessary means: she earned enough for the family to live on by doing business with the gentiles, and my grandfather Nakhum earned extra on the side. My grandfather's desire to build mills and machinery had long ago driven him from the shtetl, just as the Romani woman had predicted. For several years he had gone off to various faraway places in an effort to find somewhere to invent some sort of unusual mill. He was never successful, however. The bigger his plans grew in his head, the worse his luck turned out to be. And whenever he did build a mill in some place or other, it invariably didn't go well, and he would lose his health along with his money. After such a venture he would renounce the entire business. Instead, he would hole himself up somewhere in a large city, plant himself down as a tutor for three or four years, and earn a few hundred rubles. And so it would go, until the life of a melamed became odious to him. At that point, he would once

again go out to hunt down a mill and devise new machinery for it, until everything fell apart again. This
is how he lived out his entire life; the losses from his
mills made him miserable.

Nonetheless, however badly his business ventures
went, he did send a huge amount of money when my
grandmother wrote him that people were proposing
matches for their daughter Sarah. In short, what happened is that no less than six hundred rubles arrived
at their home in the shtetl. You just can't imagine—
my grandmother was afraid to go out in the street;
she thought people would devour her with their eyes.
Moreover, how does one store so much money? Her
father-in-law advised her to put the money in a pot
and bury it in the ground, but that seemed like a
small-shtetl approach to someone like her from the
big city. She decided to hang the money in a pouch
around her own neck, and she wore it that way until
she arranged the match and pledged the dowry.

The large dowry brought yet another advantage
to the prospects for this pretty and talented young
woman: a lot of potential grooms showed up for her,
but my grandmother disregarded their wealth. What
she wanted was pedigree and knowledge of Torah.
Even the age of the groom played only a minor role
for her; she was looking for her ideal, and she could
find that in an old man as well as a young one. Then
God provided the ideal she sought, not in an old man,
but in a young widower of thirty years with only one
child. My grandmother could absolutely not imagine

a better groom. He was a local man from our shtetl, and the son of the rabbi. What could be better?

The rabbi, my paternal grandfather Yaakov, was a great man. Aside from being a renowned scholar, he came from a very distinguished family. He had a written genealogy that showed that he was descended from a lineage listed in the *Seder Hadoros*, the eighteenth-century chronology. Despite his pedigree and his reputation as a Torah master, he conducted himself without ceremony. He felt it was just fine to stand around and chat with some tot in the road or even with a woman. The shtetl's other homeowners disparaged him because of this, and particularly in later years, Sarah couldn't bear that her father-in-law, the rabbi, didn't know how to conduct himself with dignity.

Rabbi Yaakov had another weakness, that he used to give in to his second wife, my step-grandmother. His wife, the rebbetzin, was very pretty and religious, but she was not a nice person. She was always stylish and went around impeccably dressed. She said she did this as a religious obligation. The greatest mitzvah, she said, is for a woman to dress herself beautifully and sit opposite her husband, so he could look at her and keep his thoughts pure from other women. The rebbetzin told the women in our shtetl that they should do the same, but they didn't listen to her. Our lives aren't so tranquil, they said; we have other things to do! But even if his wife had been more like the other women, she would still have had problems, because from the perspective of the shtetl, her husband didn't live at all well.

My grandfather Yaakov had a lot of problems with his wages, which were the magnificent sum of 150 kopecks, or one and a half rubles, a week—and even those kopecks would arrive for him in adversity, because of the feuds between our shtetl's homeowners that were vented at him as their rabbi. He often could not even read Torah for the Shabbes services, because they wouldn't pay his wages. Nonetheless, in spite of his problems, my grandfather had a very upbeat demeanor. It seems that the bitterness of his livelihood had very little effect on him, or perhaps he used to find consolation in his studies. One way or another, he was satisfied, and his wife was even more so. She knew only that she was supposed to shine, and everything around her was supposed to shine too. Looking at the rebbetzin, everyone thought: this woman was born to be a queen. When anyone saw her in the street in her silk bonnet with its long ribbons in the back, with her dangling earrings and her nice black wig, neatly combed, and wearing a green apron, which would stand out nicely against the black of her dress—if they met her, with her erect bearing and her beautiful face, they would unconsciously give a little bow. Whenever I looked at her, I would think that her daughter-in-law, my mother Sarah, was just like her. I couldn't imagine my mother any other way.

Just as his wife made me think of my mother, so did my grandfather Rabbi Yaakov remind me of our patriarch Abraham. He was handsome, with a long gray beard, and he had black eyes with long, bushy eyebrows. He had a good physique and was tall and stout, with an erect bearing. Moreover, in addition to his appearance, he was a good person, truly pious and sincere. In spite of his poverty, he was generous, and he would regularly invite the poor to his home on Shabbes. In short, he had the same qualities as Abraham the patriarch.

And so my grandmother Feyga arranged a match with the extraordinary Rabbi Yaakov and took his best son, Ber, as a son-in-law. Everyone expected Ber to inherit the rabbi's royal seat; in fact, people said that he was worthy of sitting on a throne in an even larger place than our shtetl. This was a man with a rare head, with great, noble feelings and a good heart. He was familiar with all the secrets of the Torah, he embodied all the characteristics of the rabbinical sages in the Gemara, and he wanted to understand thoroughly all the opinions of our great Jewish scholars.

Ber labored over his Torah. He was a great devotee of religious texts, and he had a large library. He studied day and night. He wanted to know the world's secrets so much that in his later years, he even busied himself with kabbalah, though its esoteric mysticism completely bewildered him. He was not only interested in the writings of our Jewish sages, rabbis, and kabbalists, but also in secular matters and in the sages from other peoples. He never learned any other languages, because the conditions of his life never allowed him to formally study anything other than Torah, but nonetheless he knew about secular matters, because he took an interest in everything. He was familiar with the philosophy of the ancient Greeks and also with the poppycock of later philosophers. He knew history, and not just of his own people, but also of all the great nations. He sought knowledge and truth everywhere. He esteemed truth more than anything, and he was not afraid to tell anyone what he thought. He sympathized with all who suffered. He hated wealth and "respectability"; he valued the poor the same as the wealthy.

With his vast knowledge and such exalted feelings, a man like Ber should have been able to accomplish a lot for himself and for the world, but instead, he had to resort to tutoring for one hundred rubles a term. One has to grieve about all the Jewish talent that was wasted in those days. Today, such a man would occupy a completely different place. Jewish talent still perishes even now, but we have the consolation that we are no longer to blame: we want to learn, but we are not allowed. It used to be the other way. Back then, the secular world implored us to learn, and we Jews didn't want to, since it was unseemly for a respectable child to study anything other than Torah. This is how it was for Ber when my grandmother Feyga selected him as a son-in-law for her oldest daughter Sarah; he remained trapped with all his knowledge and all his abilities in a narrow, unhappy Jewish life.

When all was said and done, my grandmother had made a good match. She paid a dowry of three hundred rubles and took in her son-in-law, providing room and board for the couple for two years, so that Ber could continue his studies. She had the most beautiful clothes made for Sarah, sewn in the city, and she put on a lavish wedding. The whole shtetl was jealous that she had attracted such a son-in-law. The bride, as was the custom, did not know the groom well, but she was of course pleased to marry him. She was an arrogant person, and her strongest desire was to have others esteem her as someone who stood above the masses; now she prided herself that she got the rabbi's son, that great scholar, and that she herself would someday be a rabbi's wife. Sarah knew that everyone was jealous of her, and it was broadly understood that her entire family would be elevated because of her father-in-law's pedigree. She was pleased with the whole situation.

Sarah didn't think much about her own inner happiness, though she must have wanted to be happy in her own home, as well as in public. But the happiness that was on display to others was much more important to her than the happiness that no one else would witness.

Sarah was a smart person but very proud, a true aristocrat. She had always considered herself better than anyone in the shtetl, because she was pretty, smart, talented, and from a respectable family; to this was added the pride that in her nineteenth year, the rabbi had chosen her as a daughter-in-law, when he could have chosen anyone. She had a way of playing down her haughtiness as if to behave in a simple way, but one could easily recognize it in her bearing. She would chat with the most ordinary person, and on the surface, it seemed as if she were behaving as an equal to him, but she managed to do so in such a way as to make everyone realize the difference in their rank. By talking to someone ordinary, she wanted to elevate him, not lower herself; she wanted to do that person a favor.

She never had friends who were her equal. She didn't want to associate with her cousins, since in their eyes she came from the same world, of course, and she couldn't do them any favors with her friendship. She therefore did better to look for a friend of lower rank, and she found one in Eydl, one of the daughters of a humble man who taught girls for a living.

Eydl was a nice girl with a good heart. Her family belonged to the petite bourgeoisie, and she was very grateful to her aristocratic friend for even associating with her. Eydl knew how to value the relationship and was in all things loyal and devoted; nothing and no work was too difficult for her. In return for her loyalty, Sarah granted this girl her friendship, and Eydl's social standing rose. Whether they truly loved each other, no one could tell, but by all appearances, they were the best of friends. They would go as a pair to a wedding, and neither would dance without the other; indeed there were few lucky women who were given the honor of dancing with them. The two of them used to even dress the same, however hard this proved to be for Eydl. One time she worked for an entire summer in a nobleman's fields, baking in the sun all day and sleeping under the open sky at night, just to earn enough money to make herself a dress like her rich friend.

One time when Eydl got some money, the two of them traveled to Rabinsk before the holidays, and they both had beautiful dresses made. The dresses were really something, because they had been made with the first sewing machine in the city. When Sarah and Eydl brought them back to the shtetl, everyone came running to see how they had been sewn. The two of them described every little detail about the machine, which they had seen with their own eyes; how one sewed with it and how it made stitches all by itself. One can imagine how important they seemed because of this, and especially Eydl. How could Eydl not cherish her friend, who exposed her to such new-fangled things, and who made her seem so privileged to everyone else!

Sarah really did Eydl a lot of favors. She did not forget her poor friend after she herself was married, and she subsidized Eydl's wedding. She also saw to it that Eydl made a match with a fine man and not with some crude youth. When Eydl got married, Sarah dressed her in her own wedding dress, and the morning after, Sarah sent her friend a *sheytl*, a marriage wig, and one of her dresses, so she wouldn't be embarrassed in front of her in-laws. She also loaned her a feather comforter for a whole year, because she didn't have any bedding. Poor thing, she really had nothing for her marriage, but nonetheless she wed a Talmud student, the son of a respectable man. Of course, none of this was easy for her. They were standing in front of the chuppah when her father-in-law caught wind of the fact that the fifty rubles dowry was missing, as was the tallis, the prayer shawl they were promised, so he grabbed his son and left. But here my grandmother Feyga intervened as a peacemaker, together with her entire household. They pledged the dowry, someone donated a tallis, Sarah brought a white tablecloth with honey cake and brandy, and they got the couple back under the chuppah and celebrated the marriage.

Life afterward equalized the two friends. In their home lives, Sarah was unhappy, and Eydl just the opposite. But the two retained their distinct views; Sarah kept her genteel perspective, and Eydl remained common. I know this from the following story: some years later, when Eydl was living in the city and her husband was off in America, he sent her a hundred dollar bill. She was so happy, she didn't know what to do. She wore the bill around her neck and examined it every day, just to see what it looked like. At the time, Sarah was passing through the city where Eydl lived, and by chance she needed fifty rubles for a few days, not out of hardship, but for business. But her friend didn't want to lend her the money. Eydl asked afterward, how could she ask for such a huge thing from her? Sarah was not angry about the incident, however. She excused her friend on the account that she had never before seen so much money and was therefore not able to part with it. Was this not behavior fitting for nobility?

And so the beautiful, smart, and talented aristocrat Sarah married the rabbi's son Ber, the scholar and expert, the idealist.

Sarah and Ber seemed destined for success as a couple, but they came from two singularly different worlds. Sarah guarded her social standing and behaved haughtily because of it, and she worked to attain her goal of rising above the masses and shining among them. Ber had a completely different character and a completely different perspective. He did not value his pedigree at all; on the contrary, he wanted all Jews to be equal. He abhorred pride and envy; in his opinion, the rabbi and the gabbai and the poor and the simple were all the same. He thought only about how to help the needy.

In Ber's mind, nothing stood higher than Torah. He never thought about money and he didn't seek out riches; he worked only to earn a livelihood. Whenever he had free time, he would sit and study. He certainly had plenty of material to study, because he spent his entire dowry on books; he got a lot more enjoyment from them than from having nice furniture in his house. He was happy to live in a modest home, as long as there were plenty of books lying around, and a good friend with whom he could talk about Torah and higher matters in general.

Ber never thought about his own happiness. He thought only about lofty matters, about how humanity could achieve something, so that people could live better and more happily—and not so much all of humanity, but specifically his own people. He was a Zionist then, back before anyone ever talked about Zionism. I figured this out years later from a book he had started writing but left unfinished. It's easy to see from his book how much he loved his people and his ancient homeland, and how he lamented the destruction of Zion and his people. His only wish was to see our Holy Land. These were the things Ber thought about at a time when he was barely earning a living. His beautiful young wife Sarah, who strived to attain wealth and respectability, suffered with their poverty and hid it so that no one would know. For her proud nature, being the object of pity was intolerable; she would have died rather than for anyone to pity her.

It's easy to imagine what kind of life they had, where the husband was a scholar who sat and thought about lofty matters, and who was a democrat through and through who thought only about the public good; and the wife was a proud aristocrat who dreamed about wealth and respectability. These two people were as far apart from each other as if they had come from different corners of the planet, but they had to live as one and spend their years together. They were the unhappiest couple in the world. Their lives were a constant struggle between two strong characters, neither of whom wanted to yield to the other. And so they fought their entire lives, and neither changed the other.

A huge part of their conflict also had to do with the boy from Ber's first marriage, who was seven years old when he arrived at his stepmother's. He came to be a very rebellious child. He was smart, but didn't want to study or obey his parents, and the older he grew, the worse it got. His father suffered a lot because of him; he lost his health trying to make him into some kind of man. His stepmother also suffered because of him, but she did not treat him well; she took out her frustrations on the boy. This may be why he behaved so badly, because he was punished so severely for every little thing. He was as afraid of the home as he was of fire, and when he avoided coming home, things got even worse: he fell in with a bad crowd and got into trouble. By the time he was fourteen, everyone was exhausted with him. His father's moralizing and his stepmother's punishments hadn't helped or changed his behavior. Ber saw that things were bad, so he did just what a man with a free and high spirit would do: he handed him over to a tailor so he could learn a trade. What pluck, in those days, that one should befoul such a pedigree by giving a child to a craftsman! But this of course did not sit well with his proud stepmother. It was beneath her dignity for her own children to have a brother who was a simple craftsman, so she fetched him back from the tailor and sent him away to a yeshiva. This annoyed his father, but he didn't interfere on his account any more. Later there were still more problems with him, and so this boy also poured a bitter venom into the beaker of poison that this couple drank from for the rest of their lives.

And this same unhappy couple that I've been describing here: these were my parents.

2

Early Memories

I was my parents' second child. From the beginning, they loved me as an only daughter, and I was fortunate to remain as such. My parents adored me because I wasn't born until eight years after their marriage, and also because I was a girl. I was a cherished present for my mother, who had lost her first child, a boy, and even more of a treasure for my father, who had never yet had a daughter. After me, my mother gave birth to two more sons.

My brothers and I did not make our parents' relationship any happier, however, and their life together continued to be just as difficult with us as it had been earlier without us. They both had strong personalities, and they fought constantly; neither wanted to concede anything to the other. Perhaps they really did love each other, but their temperaments were so incompatible that they made each other miserable. My grandmother even advised them to get a divorce, but they scoffed at the idea; from their perspective, divorce seemed bizarre and unnatural. Whether they didn't want to separate because they truly loved each other, or because of us children—who knows? With time, perhaps they would have reconciled with each other, but this was not destined to be. Death already had his plans in motion, and once Death entered our home, he didn't want to leave. He settled in with us until he had cleaned out the family, one by one. Death deprived me of my father, my mother, and my brothers, until only I was left, like a stone, all alone.

My father contracted typhus and died when he was forty-three. He left behind my thirty-two-year-old mother and three young children: I was five, my brother was three, and my baby brother was nine months. My father was ill for six weeks, during which time he used up nearly all of his thirty-four rubles in assets. Only four rubles were left for his widow and their three little children.

My father died peacefully; he was not concerned that he had not provided for his wife and children. When my mother asked him if he regretted finding himself so suddenly on his deathbed, he answered that he was very sorry, because there was still a lot that he had not learned; aside from that, he wasn't disturbed. When she pressed him further, and asked him to whose care he would leave his wife and children, he answered calmly, "To God!" He had a powerful God indeed, to be so serene in the face of death!

And so my father died, leaving behind a young wife and three small children, an older son who still had need of him, and an old father, a rabbi who had hoped to leave his son in his place after his own death. My grandfather, Rabbi Yaakov, took the blow stoically. He truly was like Abraham the patriarch, who would have slayed his only son to abide by God's will. Just like Abraham, my grandfather gave his sacrifice calmly; he didn't shed a single tear. All he said was, "Thank you, God, for the present you gave me for forty-three years. I must not have been worthy of having him any longer."

Everyone cried when my father died, except my grandfather and me. My grandfather did not cry out of piety and I—out of foolishness. I was very young at the time, and I did not understand the calamity.

I barely remember my father. I remember only one scene from my childhood when my father was still alive, but that memory remains vivid even now. I remember waking in the night and seeing a smoky little lamp burning on our huge, Russian-style heating oven, and a book lying open beside the lamp. A tall, dark-haired man with bushy eyebrows was standing there, leaning over the book. The house was almost completely dark—the lamp illuminated the book and nothing else—but even so, I remember everything quite clearly, except for the figure that stood leaning over the book, whom I see as if through a fog. This was my father, who stood absorbed in his thoughts. Who knows what deep ideas were floating around in his head at that moment?

I remember one final scene from my early childhood, but only as if in a dream. My father was stretched out on the floor, and our home was full of crying people. As much as I want to remember what was going through my little head at the time, I can't. It seems to me that I looked on the whole scene as a kind of a farce. I must have thought that my father was going away somewhere, because a few days later, I asked my mother, "When is Papa coming back?" I can't remember how she answered. That whole time feels like a dream to me. All I know is that after my father's death, my mother was left with a capital sum of only four rubles.

By the time my father died, my mother's mother, Feyga, had moved far away to the big city of Rishelevsk in the south of Russia; my grandfather Nakhum had sent for her and their children. My mother was the only member of her family who remained in Bulin, where she and my father expected him to inherit the rabbinate. My grandfather Nakhum had then died in Rishelevsk before his time—the business with the mills had shortened his life—but my grandmother and the rest of her children remained there. My grandmother longed for her home, since she hated the licentiousness of the city, but she remained in Rishelevsk for the sake of her children; they had a better life there with more opportunities than they would have had in our muddy shtetl.

When my grandmother heard the sad news about my father, she and her children came back to Bulin to help. They began to make plans for my mother. Her siblings advised her to leave the shtetl and go with them to the city, where they would get her settled, but my mother did not agree to this arrangement. First, she did not want her brothers to have to support her. She did not like to rely on anyone, and she was too proud to take favors from anyone, even her own brothers. Second, she was fearful of the city, and she did not want her children to lose their sense of Jewishness as they grew up. She was most concerned about her boys. What would become of them there? she wondered. They would certainly not be as religious as they were back at home. She had the example of her brothers. They would certainly have become rabbis if they had stayed in White Russia, and even my grandmother had abandoned this ideal for them.

These were the reasons my mother did not want to move to Rishelevsk. I don't know if this was the best decision; for me at least, it was definitely not good. But my mother was content, especially because in the shtetl, she didn't have to depend on anyone for anything. Her brothers gave her the house they had inherited from their father Nakhum, which he had inherited from their grandfather; this was a family seat that had been passed from one generation to the next. In addition to the house, her brothers gave her two hundred rubles to settle a debt from the past.

My mother used the money from her brothers to open a store in our home. The store had every kind of merchandise imaginable. My mother was so capable she could do anything, and the store did well right from the start. In addition to the store, she started a bakery and sold rolls, honey cake, and other such things that she made herself. As if that weren't enough, she also took up sewing. She sat up all night and sewed shirts for the gentiles, which she sold for twenty kopeks each. In short, she never rested; she did anything she could to earn an honest living. She didn't have many daily expenses back then. We children were still small, there was no rent to pay, we had a garden that grew enough produce to last the entire year, and we did not live large. And the store did well; within three years, my mother had saved enough money to expand. In the shtetl, people began to say that my mother was wealthy, and relatives even worried about her success, as if it might attract the evil eye. My mother was pleased with her situation and especially that she did not have to move; she could stay in her own home, where she had been born, raised, and married, and where she had given birth to her own children. She was also gratified that she was self-sufficient and could support herself and her children.

How my mother used to thank God for every kopek that she earned! I remember once, when Shabbes was over and the fire was lit, she sold some things to a Christian customer of hers for a couple of rubles. My mother went straight into the house and told an old aunt of hers, "Look here, aunt, even if I had the best brother, would he remember to send me two rubles as soon as Shabbes was over? Oh, no! But God is good and doesn't forget anyone!" And she lifted her beautiful dark eyes to the heavens and said, "Oh, thank you, God!"

As long as I live, I will never forget how my mother thanked God for giving her a livelihood. Oh, my dear, devout mother—why did God take you from me so soon? If you were still alive, I would better understand your absolute faith, your reverence and your many acts of charity, and your precious, true personality. How I wish I could see your beautiful self again, looking at us with devotion, with an expression both kind and intelligent. We children felt your love deeply. You did not display it to us openly, but we felt it anyway! I still feel your gaze on me, and even now it protects me from transgressing and desecrating the Sabbath. Even if my thoughts are not pious, I still believe in God, dear Mama, just as you did. You showed your belief openly to God and performed mitzvahs as the Torah directed. My own belief is locked in my heart; I cannot show it openly the way you did. I'm not sure why this is. Perhaps if you lived in today's world, you would be just like me. Or perhaps you were simply smarter than I am, and you understood God better than I do.

I am not clever enough to understand God. I want to know how to serve him, and I do try, wholeheartedly, according to my own limited understanding. I feel in myself the God of truth, of justice, of mercy; I am a Jewish woman body and soul. But my head is full of questions about all kinds of things that I cannot understand and that no one has been able to explain to me. I've spoken to many wise people about these issues, and to old people whom I respect. Don't ask questions, they say; what will be, will be; the world did not begin with us, and it will not come to an end with us. But I cannot be so casual about these things. The questions keep popping up, and because no one can answer them, I've begun to look at a lot of things concerning faith from a different perspective. I feel like I am losing my conviction. Of course, I do not act on my impious thoughts, which my mind tries to convince me aren't really sins. I protect myself against such transgressions, dear Mama, because I feel your pure, wise eyes on me, which vanquish all these notions. Oh Mama, I want to feel your pious gaze on me forever, to feel you here with me, my dear. Even now I can see you thanking God our Creator for providing for you and your children; your eyes light up with gratitude. But even with the appreciation that filled your heart every day, you were not destined to live for long.

3

My Education

It was only three years after my father had died, and his passing was still very much on my mother's mind, when Death returned to take another soul from her little household. My mother was left to mourn her younger son Nakhumke, a beautiful child who was four years old and gifted beyond his years. How terrible his death was! He was playing and dancing in the store; suddenly he spotted a flask of concentrated vinegar and, wanting a drink, he gulped down the poison. He ran to our mother, his mouth open and burning, but unfortunately she didn't know what to do or how to save him. She called out, but no one else knew what to do either; no one understood that fire should be quenched with water. In the meantime, Nakhumke was getting worse by the minute. Someone ran to fetch Khone the healer.

Khone had no formal training, but he was the shtetl's only medical practitioner, and they waited for him to come and save the child. But Khone didn't know any more than anyone else. He walked in, examined Nakhumke, and ordered them to come to his home with a flask, which he would fill with almond milk to give to the sick child, a spoonful every half hour. And this was the medicine that was supposed to save my brother, with his burned intestines. A crowd gathered at his bed and watched him writhe in agony. He cried for someone to save him; he was burning inside, he said, please give him something to drink. But no one gave him even a drop of water, because who cares what a child wants? If they were supposed to give him water, then Khone the healer would have ordered it. They followed Khone's instructions carefully, while the poor child suffered from his burns, and he continued to suffer for several hours, until he began to spit up pieces of flesh. As soon as our mother saw this, she quickly hired a pair of horses and left with my brother for the doctor in Seltz.

The city of Seltz was about six miles from our shtetl. It took several hours to get there, however, and before they arrived, Nakhumke died in the arms of our unlucky mother. She would not set him down; she clasped the dead child to her breast.

Our wretched, wretched mother! She embraced her child and sensed that he had fallen silent, that he was no longer moaning, that he was already cold. A cold shiver ran up her spine, and her scalp tingled. She felt a presence taking her child from her, but no, she still had him, and she held him even tighter. She consoled herself with his body, her own flesh and blood, and thought that no one could take him away from her: she had carried him under her heart, brought him into the world, suckled him, and raised him—all this she had done. She wept. Now, while it was still night, she could delude herself that he was sleeping; she clung to the hope that her child would wake up when they arrived in the city. When morning came, he would open his eyes, and the doctor would come and quickly bring him some relief.

My mother struggled with her thoughts until the coachman drove up to the cemetery, when she came to and shrieked, "Reb Moyshe, where are you taking me and my child? Take me to the doctor, or call him here!"

She sent for a good, well-known doctor, who came right away. The doctor examined the body and listened to our mother tell what had happened, how they had tried to save him, and how it hadn't helped. She begged him with tears in her eyes and told him she would pay him whatever he wanted, but he had to revive her son. By then, Nakhumke had already been dead for two hours. The doctor shook his head and said, "Your child has died. He could have lived, if only there had been someone to save him, a doctor or a proper medic. But what can one do with these small shtetls, that are so backward?"

And so the doctor denounced my mother while attributing all the problems of the miserable, uncivilized shtetls to their residents, who didn't understand that they needed a good medic far more urgently than they needed to build a third shul so the fancy homeowners wouldn't have to pray together with the simple tailors and shoemakers. With these few words, he dismissed her summarily, glanced at the sacrifice she had brought, and departed calmly, without acknowledging my mother's own suffering.

The doctor's words brought home to my mother where she was and what had just happened. She looked at her dead child. Just yesterday, he had been talking and laughing; today he lay still, his limbs immobile, as if frozen. Yesterday, his eyes had been full of life and joy, and today they were extinguished. She stayed, looking at him in misery, until someone came and told her that he needed to be buried. Only then did she realize that they were really going to take away her son. She lifted her beautiful eyes to the heavens and cried out, "Oh God, why did this happen to me? Surely I have not sinned so terribly against you! Why are you punishing me like this?" And she fell upon the child in tears.

Someone lifted my mother from her dead child and set her in the wagon. During the ride home, she grew calmer. She probably told herself that this was God's will, and that one doesn't question God. When she arrived home, deep in her own thoughts, she sank to the ground and read the *toykhekhe*, the frightening descriptions in the Torah of all the calamities and curses that the Jews would incur if they disobeyed the divine will of God.

A couple of months passed. My mother finally stopped crying, but her eyes turned darker and seemed not to shine as they once had, though of course she remained very pretty.

Her good friends could not see her distress and began to coax her to remarry. What kind of life is this? they asked. The best matches were proposed for her, and rich and distinguished men courted her. But my mother was not the kind of person who could marry twice. How could she remarry, when she was bound to our father forever through her children? She could not break that holy and eternal bond just because she might have some number of good years ahead of her.

And so my mother decided to put the happiness of her children ahead of her own. She had an important purpose in life: her husband had left her as guardian of their children, who were their assets, their flesh and blood. She had to educate them and raise them properly.

When she renounced the idea of marrying a second time as an affront to her husband and her children, I thought she was wonderful. Oh, my dear, tender mother! There was a reason my father had been so serene before he died: he had known that she could be not only a mother but also a father to his children.

My mother was very involved with our education. She didn't spare any money in engaging the best melamed in our shtetl for my little brother, who was very smart. Everyone had realized his aptitude when our father died and he learned to say kaddish, the mourner's prayer. He was only three years old then, but by the second time through, he had already mastered it.

As was traditional, he would continue to say kaddish three times a day for the next eleven months. When he spoke, all the men in the shul marveled, and tears flowed down the cheeks of the women.

My mother entrusted my own education to Mikhoel the melamed, who together with his wife rented a room and lived with us for seven rubles a year. My mother paid him 150 kopecks tuition a term, or one and a half rubles, and he tutored me at eight o'clock in the evening after teaching the young boys at cheder.

Mikhoel the melamed was a tall, thin man with a long black beard. He was pale, because he would eat meat only on Shabbes; his teaching profession wouldn't support the expense of more than that. He was an honest man and never owed anybody a kopeck in his life. If he ever did borrow money from anyone, that person would not have to remember, because they knew that Mikhoel would be sure to repay the debt. I myself saw one time when he stopped a gentile in the street and gave him a penny that he owed him. The gentile burst out laughing and told him that he had never seen such a foolish Jew.

Mikhoel's wife, Basia-Reyzl, always used to sit and spin, or pluck feathers. She and her husband had a very good life together; neither of them ever had anything bad to say about the other. They had gotten married when they were fifteen, and he used to tell how she had given him a dowry of two rubles and a barrel of wine. Now they had been together for forty years and had married off four children, but they still lived like a young couple; they couldn't take their eyes off one another. I used to be amazed that they could sit gazing at each other, grinning like children, always content to be together and talking and amusing themselves like two little doves. What did they talk about, their huge business ventures? Sometimes when I watched them sit and talk, I got the feeling that their eyes spoke even more than their mouths; their mouths just smiled. Such simpletons, I used to think, that they got such enjoyment from sitting together and gazing into each other's eyes!

But there was one thing that they did fight about: about the world to come, and more specifically, about fulfilling their obligation to give to charity. Mikhoel said that when Basia-Reyzl made a donation, this really counted as a mitzvah for him, because he had earned the money. She couldn't stand that. Basia-Reyzl said that giving to charity should count for them both, and if the mitzvah counted only for him, then she didn't want to donate any more. She always begged him to let her contribute for herself. He insisted that a Jewish woman needed no more than her three standard mitzvahs: kindling the Shabbes and festival lights, keeping a kosher home, and following the laws governing purity and intimacy. If she took care of her three mitzvahs, she would secure her place in the world to come. Basia-Reyzl let herself be persuaded. Nonetheless, she secretly set aside small change and donated it to charity; this she considered to be for herself, because her husband didn't know about it.

And so this couple, who lived with us for seven years, helped bring me up. Mikhoel taught me how to read Hebrew, and Basia-Reyzl taught me how to wash dishes. I loved them both very much, and they have a special place in my heart even today. But there came a time when I had to part from Mikhoel the melamed and go to a more advanced teacher.

I was nine years old then and very grown up. I could sell anything, and I helped my mother in the store like a good little clerk; I also swept the house, wiped down the benches, and peeled the potatoes. There were only two things that were too difficult for me to do: milking the cow and washing my own hair.

I was eager to start learning how to write. I had already learned how to pray with Mikhoel, and there was nothing more he could teach me.

In our shtetl, there were not many mothers who wanted their daughters to learn how to write. "What good is writing for a girl, anyway?" they said. "Should she note down how many grains of barley to throw in the pot?" They were of the opinion that, if a girl could knit a sock, sew a shirt, and make bread, then she was prepared; their narrow lives didn't require any more. Moreover, if she could also pray a bit and read a *tkhine*, a women's prayer, in its old-fashioned Yiddish, then she should be secure with regard to God too. She'd be able to entreat him to her heart's content.

But there were two women who did want their daughters to know how to write. One of those was Golda-Leah, the richest woman in the shtetl, the wife of Aharon Rokhes. Because she had grown up in the big city of Rabinsk, Golda-Leah could write a bit and do a little math. Her husband was a lumber merchant, and she herself ran a dry goods store that boasted some three hundred rubles of merchandise, and perhaps even more.

The other woman who wanted to give her daughter a better education was the shtetl's rich widow, my mother. My mother wanted me to know how to write, and not just Yiddish, but also Hebrew, and even Russian. She didn't think much of Russian; for a girl, she said, it was enough to know how to write down an address. But she thought very highly of Hebrew. She fantasized about her only daughter achieving greatness through her knowledge of the holy language and hoped to see me elevated above the other shtetl girls as the only one with this ability. In her own youth she had envisaged rising from obscurity and achieving some kind of illustrious life, but this was not to be her destiny. She therefore transferred her own hopes onto her children; she wanted them to achieve what she herself was not able to. In her piety, she believed that given all of the troubles in her life, God would grant her good children, and indeed, there were already indications of this. Her son was the best student in cheder, and Mikhoel told her that I also had a good head. Such a shame, my mother would say, that she was a girl; if she had been a boy, she would have certainly grown up to be a great rabbi.

And so my mother soon arranged to send me to Oreh the melamed to be taught Hebrew and to study Tanakh. In fact, I suddenly had two teachers: Oreh the melamed for Tanakh, and Nekhemiah the tutor for Yiddish and Russian. Nekhemiah used to give me an hour from two to three in the afternoon, and Oreh at eight o'clock at night, when I used to study with Mikhoel.

Nekhemiah was a tutor who taught girls how to write. He was a young man and a Maskil, a modern intellectual, who brought Abraham Mapu's popular novel, *The Love of Zion*, to our shtetl from Minsk; this was one of the first novels written in Hebrew. Nekhemiah could write Russian, and he could also speak a little. He said *da* all the time when he spoke, and because of this, people called him "The Russki." He also spoke Yiddish differently, saying "yes" instead of "yeah" like everyone else. Furthermore, he went around dressed something like an aristocrat. His mother, little Khashke, could hardly bear it, but what could she do? The poor thing had to keep quiet, because he was her only son, and as a modern man, he wouldn't have listened to her anyway, especially after he got himself a modern wife from the big city. And even if little Khashke felt strange with her "aristocratic" children, she nonetheless went away with them when they moved to Minsk, because she didn't have any way to make a living in the shtetl by herself.

Nekhemiah's departure didn't bother anyone in our shtetl except for the two rich women who wanted their daughters to learn how to write.

I have to be truthful; I was not at all happy when Oreh the melamed replaced Mikhoel as my evening teacher. I liked studying with Mikhoel much better. Something about him was more comfortable and endearing, and I was already used to him. Aside from that, I simply liked his appearance, with his erect bearing, his nice beard, and his kind way of looking at me.

Oreh the melamed was completely different. He was a thin little man with bloodshot eyes and a pale face; I thought that he never ate, because his lips were so white. He dressed poorly, and he had a tremor, which made him look cold. He seemed depressed and unhappy. He almost never laughed, and if he did ever give a little chuckle, it seemed to me that somebody must have poked him, because his eyes would quickly fill with tears. He would look as if he wanted to ask, why did you make me laugh; what do you want from me? Nonetheless, when he did laugh, he would be transformed, and his normally dull eyes would sparkle with a bit of fire. But this would last ever so briefly; the flame would be extinguished in a minute, and his two clouded, bloodshot eyes would return. There was so much sorrow and unhappiness in his face that I too felt unhappy when I looked at him. Studying with him had little appeal, and I could hardly wait for him to leave.

After our warm meal on Shabbes, I would go to Oreh's to study. He lived far from us, way over on Romani Street, in a small cottage. The cottage had three tiny little windows, but some of their panes were missing and were nailed up with boards or plugged with rags, so it was dark indoors. The heating oven, which was quite large, took up half of the cramped room, and the other half was full of their belongings: long white benches, a white table, two beds piled high with bedding, and a crib suspended from ropes. The cottage walls were black with smoke from a small lamp. The earthen floor was damp, with wastewater trickling along through it. I arrived each Shabbes to find them eating dinner on a filthy tablecloth with plates held together with wire and a bowl that had been patched and repatched. They had an assortment of spoons: two or three made of tin, and the rest of wood.

Oreh's wife and children fit right in with the squalor of their home. His wife Yente was tall and fat, with a face that was sometimes green and sometimes yellow. She could not catch her breath and wheezed with great difficulty. All kinds of melodies played from her chest, especially when she sat by herself in the smoky room with its damp floor.

This is how it was in the middle of the week, but on Shabbes, Yente would come to life. Because of Shabbes, the house was clean and dry. They ate a good dinner and rested, her husband was home, and everything seemed brighter than on other days. Something of Shabbes shone in her eyes, and from that light, Oreh's eyes became a little livelier too, and he even cracked a bit of a smile. One could see that he loved Shabbes, that he opened his home to its holiness with good food and cheer, which was otherwise unusual for him. And it turned out that the Shabbes spirit was finer there than in the most beautiful of homes, because everyone could feel it; they all cherished it. Even the pale, dejected little children were livelier; they too could feel the specialness of the day. Because it was Shabbes, they ate a good meal, which gave them the strength to eat dry bread the rest of the week. How they treasured the holy day! In a week it would return, and all would be good again, and so it would be forever and ever.

But however happy Oreh and his family felt at their Shabbes table, I was never comfortable there. I felt sorry for them, and I couldn't bear their poverty; I wanted to escape to more cheerful things. And God helped me soon enough, when the wealthy Aharon Rokhes engaged a good but expensive teacher for his children. Aharon and Golda-Leah paid him thirty-five rubles a term along with room and board, and they let him teach me too, together with their children. My mother had to cajole them to allow this, but it was an advantage to the teacher. We paid him another seven rubles, which he put to good use for his wife and four children, who all had to live on forty-two rubles a term.

My new teacher, Berl, was also pale and had sunken cheeks, but he wasn't nearly as frightening as

Oreh. Berl was clean and respectably dressed, with a nod to the German fashion. You could say that he was half from the old world and half from the new, in that he was pious, but he had a modern education. He was a Maskil, just like Nekhemiah the writing tutor, but he was better educated, and a lot smarter too. He was just as honest as Mikhoel, and he made sure not to waste any time during his lessons. He never complained. He seemed to be quite satisfied with his situation, and he looked on life with something of a smile, as if to say, is it worth the trouble to make a fuss about such foolishness as our trivial existence? He still teaches to this very day, and he still looks at the world as a philosopher.

And so I was placed under the tutelage of this teacher after having been with Oreh, whom I couldn't bear, and a new world opened up for me, a beautiful, rich world, and a bigger one, with new pleasures and new desires. From Oreh's smoke-blackened cottage, I moved to Aharon Rokhes's parlor, where the floors were painted, and there was soft furniture covered with red cotton fabric, and toile draperies hung on the windows. It was not at all like a Jewish home, but instead like that of a clergyman or a nobleman. I liked that very much. I looked at the beautiful rooms and daydreamed about getting married in a big city someday, and having a house like this, with a parlor. I remember that for the first few days after I began to study there, I was spellbound. All I could think about was the beautiful room and the toile draperies.

I felt like I was in Paradise. I never wanted to leave, and when I did, I couldn't wait to return the next day and be in this beautiful home again, to sit quietly and study and write, and not be disturbed by anyone.

I was also happy because I had a friend of my own there, someone to study with. This was Merke, Aharon Rokhes's eldest daughter. We were the same age and had the same level of knowledge, but she was luckier than me, because she had a father, and a rich one at that. Merke was pampered, and her parents let her do what she wanted. She never helped around the house, because they had a maid. She ate the best things, and she dressed beautifully, just like the Russian Orthodox priest's daughter, Sashke the *panienke*, the young lady; she went out in the middle of the week in clothes fit for Shabbes. I was very jealous of Merke. My own life was so different; I felt like an ox harnessed to a swing plow. I had to do everything at home, and I had to watch over the store, and if a gentile stole anything, my mother would give me a thrashing because I hadn't paid enough attention, because I was planning to have fun with my girlfriends. "It's time to get this foolishness out of your head!" my mother would say. "You're not a child anymore; you're already eleven years old, a young woman. Are you comparing yourself to Merke? You're not at all the same!"

And so my mother chastised me, and I felt burdened with everything. I never even got enough sleep; my mother woke me every day at seven o'clock in the morning. My eyes would still be glued shut, but I tried to wake up as I quickly dressed, and at the same time I thought how lucky Merke was that she was still asleep. "Why does she get everything, and why am I so unlucky?" I used to think as I washed my face. But I would soon forget about Merke, because my head would be full of thoughts about my lessons.

I was really annoyed that I never had time to review what we had learned, but I was free for only those three hours when I was studying with Berl. The rest of the day I had work to do at home or in the store, so there was no time for homework. I thought about my lessons constantly. Whether I was sweeping the house, peeling potatoes, or weighing a pound of flour, I was searching for everything that my brain had hidden away about the previous day's lessons. And I did well, since I wasn't totally worthless after all; once I learned something, it was mine forever. Nevertheless, my thoughts were constantly working, so I would know how to answer when my teacher questioned me. It was unthinkable for me not to be prepared. I always wanted to know the right answer, and I wanted to be praised. I was beside myself with joy when Berl smiled and told me, "Very good!"

I was a much better student than Merke, though she didn't have a poor head. But her memory wasn't as good as mine, and she also didn't want to learn as badly as I did. She simply didn't care whether she knew something or not. Our teacher scolded her and asked why she didn't study, and he always pointed out how well I was learning. I was in seventh heaven with the pleasure of doing better than Merke, and I was grateful to her from the bottom of my heart. I would quietly help her from time to time, but I would do it in such a way that our teacher would hear—deliberately, so he would give me a pat on the head and say I was a good girl, while he would scold her at the same time for relying on my kindness. In this way, I got pleasure from all sides.

And so I lived for an entire summer. Every day I had three good hours, which I still consider to be the best of my life.

4

Shtetl Life

My mother was kind and affectionate, but she didn't pamper us, and especially not me. She punished us for the smallest things, and she really made me suffer when anything went missing from our store. The gentiles in our shtetl were terrible thieves. They would steal anything, even a bagel, and every time some piece of merchandise went missing, my mother would hit me for not preventing the theft. My mother's blows provoked in me a hostility toward the gentiles. I looked at every one of them as a thief or a bandit, and I couldn't imagine that there were also honest people among them. At the time, I did not yet know the secret that all the crimes I attributed to the gentiles, they attributed exactly the same to us: they thought the Jews were bloodsuckers who exploited the Christians.

Despite my problems with the thefts, things were in many ways not at all bad for me. I had a higher standing than the other girls in our shtetl in every way; I even dressed more beautifully than any of them. When I was very small, I wore clothes that my aunt had shipped to me from Rishelevsk, and as I grew up, my mother continued to dress me well. She had very pretty dresses sewn for me in Seltz, made from colorful Russian prints, and she never brought the same fabric home to sell in our store; she wouldn't stand for anyone else to wear the same kind of clothes as me. She could have earned a good profit; someone would have snatched up the material without thinking of the expense, just to dress like me. But my mother prided herself on appearances and respectability, and with anything related to respectability, my mother did not consider money to be a factor.

At the time, I did not understand my mother. It seemed to me that if the other girls wore the same clothes as me, it would have reflected well on me, because I was the reason they all dressed so beautifully. But there were a lot of things about my mother's character that I did not understand back then, so this was just another mystery for me. Nonetheless, I followed her in every way. I wanted to be just like her, just as smart and especially just as pious.

My mother prayed by heart every day while doing all her work. I could not yet pray by heart, however, and I had no time to sit down with a prayer book during the week. And so on Shabbes, I devoted myself entirely to God. I said my morning prayers with great fervor, and I enjoyed reciting the blessing after our midday meal. But it wasn't until after the meal that I really sat down to my prayers: first the *Sedra*, that is, the weekly Torah portion, and then the kabbalistic *Nachalat Tsvi* that was popular with so many women, with its ethical passages and its stories and revelations. After this, I read the weekly chapter from the *Shevet Musar*, another popular moral treatise. In the summer, as was traditional, I read *Pirkei Avot*, the *Ethics of the Fathers*; and in the winter, *Barkhi Nafshi*, Psalm 104. To finish up, I said the afternoon *Mincha*, and, like every woman, I recited *Got fun Avrom*, and finally *Veyiten Lekha*, the closing prayer.

The celebration of Shabbes gave me the strength to get through the rest of the week. How I cherished that holy day! On Shabbes, I had everything that I lacked during the week: tranquility, sleep, good food, and the chance to go for a walk with my rich girlfriend. Above all, I was delighted to be able to read.

Reading was my entire life. I was even happy to read the moralistic *Shevet Musar* and *Kav-Hayashar*; I couldn't imagine anything better. I really enjoyed the stories about the lives of our ancestors in the Torah portion, and the *Shevet Musar* drew me in completely with its terrifying stories about hell.

In the *Shevet Musar*, I read that even at the gates of hell, you could get a glimpse of the terrible things that were taking place inside, since there were people hanging there suspended by their feet, their arms, and even their hair. These last were women who received this terrible punishment for keeping their own hair after they married, instead of shaving it off. I could imagine how wretched they were. My entire religious observance derived from my fear of hell, since I was so scared of these punishments. I imagined that the older I grew, the more pious I would become. When I got married, I would definitely be observant and make sure to fulfill all my religious obligations. I figured I would pray three times each day and not eat without reciting a blessing over the meal. Whenever possible, I would make sure to offer a hundred benedictions every day. Then I would certainly be blessed! And I would keep Shabbes and the holidays faithfully. If I become rich, I would donate Torah scrolls to the synagogues with great pomp, and I'd help the poor as much as I could.

For me, giving to charity was the best and dearest mitzvah; compared to praying, it was easy, and it was helpful. The mitzvah of praying, on the other hand, was very hard for me. Like all people, I had something like a little angel who lived inside me, my *yetzer toyv*, my natural inclination to good, who did battle with the little devil inside me, my *yetzer hara*, my inclination to evil. On Shabbes, my *yetzerim* manifested themselves in the struggle between the mitzvah of praying versus my desire to read stories. Before I began to pray each week, they carried out an entire war in my heart.

Shabbes mornings, I'd wake up calm and well rested. I'd drink a glass of sweetened chicory, made with lots of milk and topped with a fat layer of *penka*, the milk skin, which my mother had made for me before she left for shul. At home, it was clean and quiet, and I'd be free from gentiles and thieves; it would feel so good. Since I could experience such a nice day only once a week, I wanted to fill it with pleasurable activities: gadding about, strolling in the Yashtsikover forest, or reading a nice story from the little books that my grandmother the rebbetzin had given me. My grandmother had a whole library; there weren't any novels, God forbid, but there were lots of wonderful books with descriptions and tales about Orthodox rabbis, *tsaddikim*, and Hasidic rebbes.

I was fascinated with these stories, and I could hardly wait for Shabbes so I could read them. Of course, one mustn't forget about God, so before anything else, I tried to start with the *korbn-minkhe*, the women's prayer book. But my *yetzer hara* wouldn't let me. He'd tell me that the stories were better than praying, and that a little girl like me was simply not yet obligated to pray. Besides, he asserted, who would know whether I had prayed or not? My mother wasn't even there; I could tell her whatever I wanted. With this in mind, I'd set aside the *korbn-minkhe* and pick up a book of stories . . . but then I'd spot the *Shevet Musar* and remember the bitter suffering of the wicked people who were tortured in hell. My heart would start to pound, and a cold shiver would run down my spine. At this point, my *yetzer toyv* would show up and tell me how good it was to pray, to serve and praise God, and he said that if I did so, I'd be worthy of the world to come. I imagined the scene in Paradise that I had read about in one of my mother's texts. I pictured a beautiful large garden with lovely fruit trees, and under every tree, a *tsaddik* sat on a golden chair beside a golden table. On each table lay unfurled a Torah scroll, and the *tsaddikim* sat and studied its mysteries, while the sky above their heads was blue and the sun shone down upon them all. In the middle of the garden stood the Tree of Life, which had so many branches that it covered the entire garden and protected all the *tsaddikim* from the heat of the sun, while the sunbeams illuminated all of its leaves. Such a delicious aroma emanated from the tree that one's hunger would be sated with it; this is why the *tsaddikim* don't have to eat in Paradise.

Every Shabbes morning, all these thoughts ran though my head while I stood next to the bookcase, holding in one hand the *korbn-minkhe* and in the other some book of stories. I'd want to set the book of stories down, but its title would draw me in to have a quick look at the first page, to see what it was about and how it began. Before long, I would force myself to set the book aside. This was what I called rejecting the *yetzer hara*; instead, I opened the *korbn-minkhe* and began to pray. It was then that I really felt good. I prayed with intention; when I said the *Shema*, I lifted my eyes toward Heaven and said the words slowly, exactly as my mother did. When I said the daily benedictions, the *Amidah*, I said the words quietly just as I had read I should do in the *Shulchan Aruch*, the *Code of Jewish Law*, standing up straight as if before a tsar and laying my hand on my chest, to show God that I was praising him with my entire heart. In those moments, I didn't think about anything but God. I felt that the *yetzer toyv* had won; he had ousted his enemy, and now he was my master. He sat with me in my heart and persuaded me to goodness, and he showed me how to be pious and honest, and how to serve God. Oh, how far my thoughts would run—far, far away, all the way to heaven, to God's throne itself, where all prayers linger and beg to be embraced. An angel would take all of these prayers and form them into a crown for the head of the heavenly King, and among all of the prayers in the crown, which glittered like diamonds, there would also shine out a tiny diamond of a prayer from an eleven-year-old girl, on whom the King of Kings would look with pleasure and rejoice.

With all this on my mind, I'd float up above the entire world and all seven levels of heaven. It felt so good up there that I wouldn't want to come back down to our foolish, sinful world, and I'd be so deeply engrossed in my thoughts that I'd have absolutely no sense of how to bring my praying to an end. When I finished the closing prayer, the *Aleynu*, I'd feel as if I had just descended from a tall, green mountain into a poor, gray valley. After a few minutes, I would start to feel normal again. I'd go out onto the porch and watch people walk home from shul, and say "Good Shabbes" to them all. And then I'd spot my mother in her blue print dress, with a silk kerchief with big flowers on it. (I still have that kerchief to this very day.) Even though she looked sad, my mother shone so brightly that one's gaze was invariably drawn to her. She rarely laughed or even smiled, but if anything, her sorrow made her beauty even more apparent.

My mother was always sad, and she didn't like it when we shouted or fooled around. My little brother, who was a real scamp, would adopt a stately demeanor when my mother was home.

Even when we were small, my mother could not tolerate our misbehavior; she expected us to have the judgment of adults. She couldn't bear to see any kind of shortcoming in us. She simply didn't want to accept that all people are flawed, and she wanted her children to be the best in the entire world.

Although she loved us as much as life itself, my mother was strict with us, and she never displayed her love openly. She never kissed us or caressed us, and she never gave us an affectionate word. This is traditional in White Russia, where mothers raise their children strictly and without warmth; they don't even try to be approachable. Their reasoning is, if their children lost their fear of their parents, it would seem like the parents were giving in to them. But what a mistake this is! These mothers do not understand that they are alienating their children, and the more they distance themselves from their children, the more their children withdraw. Their children would rather confide in strangers than in their own mothers, and the mothers don't know whether their own children are doing poorly or well. When their children are naughty, the mothers make it even worse by punishing them, which makes them misbehave even more. The entire blame of a poor upbringing lies squarely with the mothers; what they don't realize is that they could improve their children's conduct with kindness. With a kiss and a caring smile, a mother can get a child, even a naughty one, to do anything. The loving words and fervent kisses that a mother showers on her children in their early years will remain dear to them throughout their entire lives.

I remember how I would often pretend to be sick and not eat for a couple of days, so that my mother would come feel my head to see if it was hot and give me a kiss on the forehead. She would sit next to me and question me with soft, caring words to see how I was doing. I was thrilled by her presence, by her hand on my forehead and her kiss; I would feel like dancing and jumping for joy. I would do anything; I would obey my mother come hell or high water, if only she would always look at me so lovingly and kiss me like this! I would want to stay sick even longer, but I would really want to eat; besides, my heart would ache for my mother: I would see how she sat and looked at me with tears in her eyes. She would tell me that she would go call Khone the healer, which made me very afraid. I wasn't worried he would realize that I was pretending to be sick, because I was certain that he wouldn't, but on account of the bitter medicine he always gave me.

When Khone came, my mother would question him; what did he think, was it something dangerous,

God forbid? If it was anything serious, she'd go to Seltz for the doctor, she said, and the tears would flow down her cheeks. Then she'd hastily wipe her eyes and rush over to me, saying: "My child, it's time to take your medicine; you have to finish the bottle today. Khone says he'll give us another one tomorrow, and when you finish taking them both, you'll be well again."

In the meantime, I'd feel more and more unhappy: I was supposed to finish taking two bottles of bitter stuff, and for what? I was so hungry, and Khone had warned that I shouldn't be allowed to eat until I had finished all the medicine. So I would have to go hungry for another two days, and lie in bed—and all for a kiss from my mother and a pat on the head!

Even though it cost me dearly to get a kiss from my mother, I could live for months from the pleasure of having done so, until I would long for another and play the game all over again.

Oh, my dear, beloved, loyal mother, forgive me for my childish foolishness, which took such a toll on your health. I was not to blame for my nature; I just wanted to see kind, smiling faces and hear tender words, and when I did, I felt happy. Even today, someone can win me over for life by speaking kindly and being cheerful; I believe these things are connected to a good heart. What I still can't understand is how a face can smile and a mouth can say all sorts of nice things, when the heart feels exactly the opposite. I will never be able to understand this.

But my dear mother, you were smarter and more practical than I am. You understood that a good heart was more important than a cheerful face. You didn't display your love to us, but you had it hidden in your heart, like a treasure. I'm certain you thought that your children should be able to understand that you loved them more than life itself. I remember when you stopped eating meat to save money for my tuition, and how you gave us your portion instead.

Despite not being demonstrative, my mother was very involved with my life, and she did want me to enjoy myself. She even wanted me to be able to dance. She paid Khaye-Beyla, who was renowned as a dancer in our shtetl, to take me along with her to all the weddings. Of course, I was in seventh heaven with this arrangement.

Khaye-Beyla was mistress of all weddings because of her dancing; no one would even think about starting the dancing without her. Even if she didn't show up until midnight, everyone would still wait for her. Every wedding felt a little sad until she arrived, but the mood turned festive as soon as she did. The musicians would begin to play when they spotted her, because they knew her so well, and Khaye-Beyla would immediately collect money for a quadrille. There were two tiers of musicians for weddings in our shtetl, so the cost to dance depended on who was playing. When Shloyme the smith played, he charged three kopeks a dance, but the musicians from Seltz charged ten.

Some girls were not lucky enough to dance; there were those who didn't have the kopeks. I felt sorry for them, and my heart would go out to them, seeing them stand with their thirsty eyes while they watched the other women dance. But even if they had the money, they weren't guaranteed a dance, because there was so little time. At our weddings, the girls would dance only before the ceremony. Right after the ceremony, everyone would eat dinner, and after that, the men would dance. Because there was so little time for the women to dance, many would be left out, and these were usually girls who were poor, unattractive, or from the lower classes. A lot of these girls appealed to Khaye-Beyla for the opportunity to dance. She would sometimes oblige them, but she made sure that they danced separately from those with higher standing. She wanted everyone to be happy, but she really was concerned only with the rich and those with pedigree; the lower class didn't matter to her. As for me, I was always the happiest among the happy. Even though I was just a young girl, I danced with all the grownups, and what's more, with Khaye-Beyla herself; I was always her lady. Everyone was jealous of me. I noticed this, and as I passed by the other girls, I held my head high and affected a bit of arrogance, as if to say, "Look who I am!"

This pleasure of mine cost my mother some forty or fifty kopeks for every wedding, because she had to pay for Khaye-Beyla as well as me.

Khaye-Beyla enjoyed associating with me and the other pedigreed girls because she came from a very simple home herself: her father, Khayim-Dovid, was only a coachman. From time to time, a horse would die on him, and he would take up trading in mushrooms instead. But he typically did this for no more than a couple of months, because he always lost money when he engaged in commerce. Instead, he would sell off a piece of his property and buy another horse with the proceeds. He would also give Khaye-Beyla a bit of the money, and she would travel to Seltz and have a nice dress and a coat made, and buy a pair of shoes with high heels and pointy toes.

Khayim-Dovid had been married two or three times and had a lot of children. His sons were all nice; one of them had somewhat unexpectedly turned out to be a great scholar and was well on his way to becoming a rabbi. Khayim-Dovid arranged a great match for this son in Seltz with Reb Yonah the maggid, an itinerant preacher. Reb Yonah had only one daughter, who was a real pain, but there was pedigree and wealth galore in the family, and Khayim-Dovid was very smug about the match. Furthermore, he could pride himself on his talented Khaye-Beyla. She wasn't bad to look at, she could write a little, and she could sew, embroider, dance, and sing. On top of that, everyone knew she was sharp; she herself thought there was no one smarter. She made fun of everyone and slandered them all; she knew all the shtetl's secrets.

She was more arrogant than Haman, even if she was poorer than Mordecai.

Khayim-Dovid lived in a small cottage near the study hall, on a large lot right in the middle of the shtetl; that is, in the shtetl's seat of honor. The property had belonged to their family for years and passed from one generation to the next; it was all they owned and was their pride and joy. Khayim-Dovid was the first to touch his holy inheritance. He had already sold off three of the best spots from the property. But Khayim-Dovid didn't care if his garden kept getting smaller, so long as he held on to his cottage.

Inside, the cottage looked very nice, because Khaye-Beyla made sure everything was kept in good order. The walls and benches were painted white, there were curtains on the windows, and the beds were nicely made with embroidered covers. On the walls, mounted in frames, were pictures that Khaye-Beyla had also embroidered: an eagle, a songbird, a goat, a dog, and a mizrach showing the Holy Land, which hung on the eastern wall for prayers.

The cottage was warm in the winter and it was cool in the summer. It was always merry, and everyone would gather there: homeowners, coachmen, merchants, teachers, girls, young men, and young women. Everyone enjoyed themselves, laughing and talking about everything under the sun, and they stayed until late at night, especially Saturday evenings. Khaye-Beyla loved this more than anything. She mixed everywhere and involved herself with everything, and people listened to her since she was regarded as such a clever young woman.

Even though Khaye-Beyla was so talented, she had never married. She insisted that she didn't like anyone, but everyone quietly said otherwise. Meanwhile, she was already twenty-six years old, and people began to whisper in the shtetl: how long will she wait? She should go ahead and marry the shlimazel Khatzkel the Tall, the poor, unfortunate widower, who had already buried two wives in our shtetl.

Khatzkel the coachman was one of the most frequent visitors at Khayim-Dovid's. Everyone told Khayim-Dovid that he should arrange the match, but Khayim-Dovid didn't want to hear anything about it. He thought that a match with Khatzkel was too lowly for his talented daughter. But when Khayim-Dovid suddenly dropped dead, Khaye-Beyla married Khatzkel. She was given the cottage as a dowry, and everyone continued to spend time there after they married, just as before. Khaye-Beyla didn't wait around for these gatherings, however; she went out somewhere different every night to amuse herself.

I really liked Khaye-Beyla because of the weddings that she took me to. But to tell the truth, it wasn't the dancing that interested me nearly as much as the music; there was nothing I enjoyed more. As soon as I heard Shloyme's fiddle, I would go crazy with delight. It seemed to me that the fiddle itself was speaking and telling wonderful stories, even if no one was actually singing. Luckily we did have music in our shtetl: there was Shloyme the smith with his fiddle, and the gentile Ivan's son with his accordion and his folk flute, and the priest's daughters, the *panienkes*, with their grand piano. Even though the priest's piano was out of tune, my ear was not hard to please; as long as there was music, I didn't care.

I remember those happy summer nights so well, when I would stand for hours in the street and listen to the music. The moon would light up the entire shtetl, and the sky was clear and tinged with blue. All was quiet; nearly everyone was asleep already, though the gentiles were still in the tavern, and my mother would be fussing over something inside at home. But the priest's house would be lit up and merry; the *panienkes* played the piano so beautifully that no one wanted to leave. My mother would yell at me to go to bed already, since she would have to wake me up early the next morning, but I'd beg her to let me stay out a little longer. I couldn't tear myself away. I was so delighted to listen to the music while gazing at the moon. Oh, how beautiful the moon was! I would look to see if I could make out the man in the moon. If I paid close attention, I really could discern a face, but then it would suddenly vanish, and then reappear again.

I would be so lost in my thoughts, gazing at the moon and listening to the piano, that I would forget where I was. I'd be riveted to my spot, my limbs frozen. At times on a moonlit night, I'd hear Ivan's son playing his folk flute by himself, and my whole heart thrilled to its sweetness and delight. Sometimes the music would carry me off, and I would fly all the way to the man in the moon with the sounds of the piano escorting me there. If my mother had not forced me to come in, I would probably have fallen asleep outside. Long after I came inside, I would continue to gaze through the window at the beautiful, idyllic night.

I was so strongly attracted to the night and its beauty that I would even forget to be afraid of the Cold Shul, which wasn't far from our house, and which was always full of ghosts at night.

The Cold Shul was the oldest shul in Bulin; no one remembered when it had been built. Inside, it was very beautiful: the ceiling was domed and very high, and on the Holy Ark stood large, carved black birds. People prayed in the Cold Shul only on Rosh Hashanah and Yom Kippur. The rest of the year, because it was unheated, the shul remained empty, and the Torah scrolls were taken away. Without the Torah, people believed that demons had free reign in the shul; there were stories about how they danced there all night long. When people walked by the Cold Shul at night, they stuck their fingers in their ears and whispered, *"Shema Yisroel."*

One person actually saw the demons in the Cold Shul. This was Blumke, the wife of Moyshke the shammes, the caretaker. Once, at the time of the first penitential *selichos* prayer services before the High Holidays, at two in the morning, Blumke went to kindle the fire in the women's section of the Tailors' Shul.

All of a sudden, looking down the road to the Cold Shul, she saw its door open by itself, and a flood of light poured out. She saw a horde of people, women together with men, all singing and dancing, and she heard wild shrieking. Blumke felt the hair on the back of her neck stand up. She was so terrified that she completely forgot the words she was supposed to say to repel the demons. But then she remembered, and she cried out, "*Shema Yisroel!*" These words helped, and indeed, it became a little quieter; she even heard a goat bleat. Blumke figured she had chased away the demons, so she looked around a bit—and to her surprise, she saw another terrible scene: a man was standing in the doorway of the Cold Shul with his tongue sticking out. His tongue was white, and it was so long that it extended across the entire courtyard of the shul. When she saw this, Blumke choked out with a cry, "*Shema Yisroel!* Help!"

At her racket, her husband Moyshke the shammes soon showed up; he had been going around with his staff to wake everyone for *selichos*. He calmed his Blumke down, and when he went over to the Cold Shul to investigate, the man with the tongue had disappeared. "It seems that the demons only have power over women," Moyshke concluded.

Early the next morning, the entire shtetl went to inspect the Cold Shul; perhaps someone would notice some trace of the previous night's events. But no one could find anything at all. However, in the vestibule by the door of the shul, exactly in the spot where Blumke had seen the man with the long tongue, lay Oreh the melamed's white goat with several tiny kids, which she had brought into the world the previous night. At the time, there were some sages in our shtetl who had the temerity to suggest that all Blumke had seen was the goat with her white tail, and nothing more. But everyone wanted to stone them for this: what did they mean, she saw the goat and nothing more? Didn't Blumke know Oreh the melamed's goat? Who didn't know her?

And in truth, everyone did know Oreh the melamed's goat. She was the prettiest goat in the shtetl. People used to complain about her, that she didn't comport herself well. She ran through all the gardens and the yards, and she didn't even go home at night. She frequently disappeared into some place or other, but her mistress, Oreh's wife Yente, didn't worry. Yente knew that she would come home when she needed to be milked. It seemed to me that through the goat, the status of her mistress was also elevated, because everyone was always talking about her antics. Here was someone crying that Yente's goat had eaten the cabbage in the garden, and there was someone complaining that Yente's goat had drunk up all the cow's gruel. When a daughter strayed from her mother for too long, her mother would say, "She's running around, just like Yente's goat." In short, wherever there were two people, Yente's goat would make the third. And naturally, with the story about Blumke in the Cold Shul, the goat became even more famous.

Blumke got sick somewhat more often after that night, and everyone was even more afraid of the Cold Shul from then on. No one wanted to believe that the goat was to blame; they believed in the man with the long tongue. At night, everyone trembled when they walked by the Cold Shul, and children were scared to death. We lived right nearby, so we were even more afraid. But on those beautiful, bright summer nights, because of the music and the songs, I would forget completely about the Cold Shul and its terrifying visitors.

I remember those songs even now. Sometimes when I sing them, they transport me far away to the porch at our old home. I can still picture the beautiful moon with its face, and I can hear the beautiful folk flute and the grating sounds of the *panienkes* playing on the priest's discordant piano. I can even hear my mother's voice exhorting me to go to sleep. If only I could relive those happy moments from my childhood!

As I grew older, I began to realize that I was different from other girls: no one else seemed to be delighted by the moon, or the folk flute, or the priest's grand piano. One time I pointed out a beautiful sunset in the Yashtsikover forest to my friend Malke. The sky was red as the sun lowered itself behind the trees; it seemed as if a blaze of fire was burning in the woods. I was stunned that no one else had noticed, while I could not tear my eyes from the scene. I asked Malke how she liked the sunset. At first, she didn't understand what I was talking about, but when I explained as best as I could what I was feeling, she burst out laughing and said that it was good that I had told only her about this, because she would keep it a secret. If I told anyone else, they would make fun of me.

"Think about it," she said, "What a fool you are! What's so great about looking at the sun? What kind of beauty is there in it? Here is the sun like the sun's supposed to be, exactly as God created it! And besides, you're not supposed to stare at the sun, because that's where *Moyshe Rabeynu* is, Moses our Teacher, and we sinful people must not look upon his face, lest we go blind."

Malke's words made a strong impression on me. Compared to her, and from her perspective, I was very young. I did seem to be more foolish than everyone else! I had already asked her if her heart wasn't moved when she heard Ivan's son playing his folk flute and singing his beautiful songs. She had considered me a bit, then answered no, she didn't like the flute at all; she liked the new quadrille that the musicians from Seltz played a lot better. I felt a bit embarrassed and answered that I understood that the quadrille from Seltz was nicer, but I just wanted to know, why was it that when I heard the flute, my heart began to quiver, tears welled up in my eyes, and I felt so, so happy!

And how his singing stirred me! I would wonder, why do the gentile boys sing such beautiful songs, and why don't Jewish boys sing? Why are the gentiles always so merry, and the Jewish boys so preoccupied? How nice it would be, if the Jews lived in the villages and plowed, sowed, and reaped in the fields. The boys would study for half a day, and the rest of the time, they would work the land. At night, when they left the fields, they would sing the kind of songs the gentiles sang. The girls would also sing as they left the fields. Oh, I would like it so much!

When I told Malke what I was thinking, she looked at me as if I were crazy. "What do you mean?" she asked, "How can a Jewish boy sing a song and whistle on a folk flute? And how could the girls sing as they left the fields; would the men be able to hear them? What do you mean, Jewish villages, instead of shtetls? Would it be appropriate for Jews to till the land and spread manure? What are you talking about? We'd all be as ignorant as the gentiles!"

I had to concede that Malke, who at that time was already sixteen years old, had stronger arguments than I. And thus did she rout the dreams of the first Jewish colony that I, the eleven-year-old heroine, had wanted to build.

Malke could not feel all that I did because she had something of an impoverished soul; she never wondered about anything beyond what she had seen with her own eyes. In return, she was blessed with a pretty face, which for a girl is often more highly regarded than having a sublime soul anyway. Who sees a soul? But everybody sees a pretty face. Malke was not some extraordinary beauty, but she had dark blond hair and a round little face with rosy cheeks and brilliant blue eyes. Briefly put, she was pleased enough with her looks. However, she did suffer because she was quite short, and she tried everything she could to appear taller. She wore heels so high that she sprained her ankles, and when she walked around, she held her shoulders as high as she could. She'd say, "Tell me the truth—if I were a little taller, would I be beautiful?" And I would inevitably answer yes.

Malke's mother, Eydl, was my mother's poor friend from years back, whom my mother had helped with her wedding. Eydl was also troubled by her daughter's short stature, but she took comfort in her good looks. Eydl was a fervent and proud mother, and she wanted to secure nice things for her children. Like my mother, she valued respectability and pedigree. Some years back, her husband had gone to America, stayed for four years, and then returned to their home in the nearby city of Seltz. Back in the shtetl, we soon heard all about how Eydl's husband had shown up with one thousand rubles, a gold watch with a chain with gold links, a silk kerchief, and other such things. People couldn't stop talking; what would she do with all that money? In the end, she did something that surprised everyone. Eydl knew that in Seltz, no one would notice her newfound wealth; only back in the shtetl would people know who she had been earlier and what she was now. And so Eydl drove into Bulin with great fanfare. She leased a huge house and a store right in the middle of the shtetl, and she filled the store with all kinds of merchandise.

Eydl did have one concern, which was how to make a nice, pedigreed match for Malke, so as to elevate her entire family. Malke considered herself to be a real aristocrat. She wore nicer clothes than the other girls and only befriended children from respectable families. Her devotion to me was not without purpose; she had made friends with my pedigree rather than with me myself. I did not understand any of this; I truly loved her, even if I didn't know why. Perhaps if there had been a different girl in her place, I would have loved her just as well. I always wanted to show Malke proof of my love, and I wanted her to feel the same as I did about everything. More than anything, I wanted to get her to like reading, but she simply wasn't interested.

I did get her intrigued by the chapbook *The Bird of Paradise*, by the great author Shomer, a story that brought Malke to tears. If Shomer had known Malke, he would have been very pleased that his story had been able to provoke tears even in someone with such a cold soul. I too was pleased; I thought that now she would get interested in books, just like me, and we would be able to read together. But I was wrong; she just wasn't interested. I did get her to read another short story by Shomer, *The Forest Child, or the Princess in the Forest*. I hoped that I could borrow longer books from the library in Seltz, novels that

Shomer himself had written. I thought I could really get Malke hooked then, because a novel was not just some simple little chapbook. I personally wanted to read Shomer's novel, *The Convict*, which Hershke the Turk was always talking about. But *The Convict* was really hard to come by, since it was always checked out of the library. No one could get enough of it.

Since I didn't have access to any long novels, I contented myself with shorter stories. I found something of interest in each of them, and I remembered them all by heart. On Shabbes I would gather a couple of dozen girls and recite stories for them. Even older people were intrigued; sometimes on Shabbes I would sit on my Aunt Zlata's porch with quite a few women, and I would tell them stories too. For the grownups, though, I would relate completely different kinds of stories. I would tell them the moralistic stories from the *Shevet Musar* and the *Kav-Hayashar*, or what I had read in the *Bekhinat ha-Olam*, or *The Examination of the World*, the popular poem written by Jedaiah ben Abraham Bedersi after the expulsion of the Jews from France back in the fourteenth century. I found these and other such tales among my grandmother's books. More than anything, the women really liked the story of the *Gur Aryeh*, the Young Lion of Judah, and someone would always ask me to tell it again. I still remember it very well today. All the women enjoyed it thoroughly and said that when I told it, the pearls would flow from my lips, as if I were a maggid. A girl born with such intelligence, they said, was a defiance of the natural order of the world.

In Bulin, I had a reputation not only for my story-telling, but also for my letter writing. People came from all over the shtetl to ask me to write letters for them. Nobody had to tell me what to say; I understood what everybody had in mind. I even wrote a letter for a girl to her bridegroom, and it was a big hit with him. I remember that it started like this: "To my magnanimously born, tremendously illustrious fi-ancé." I have forgotten what I wrote after that, but I remember that when her bridegroom answered, he wrote that he was overjoyed that his bride could write such an intelligent letter; he had not realized that about her earlier. The bride said that she could not even imagine what kind of letter I would write to my own bridegroom, if I could write this well to a stranger. Truth be told, I did already want to experience this myself. When I wrote to some unknown bridegroom, I would imagine that I was writing to my own, and I poured my whole heart into these letters.

5

April Fools

And so I lived out my young life until I was twelve years old. I had studied with my new teacher, Berl, for one term, and was making good progress; I could already write in Hebrew, and I knew a bit of Russian. My mother said that if I completed another term with Berl, she would send me to Seltz to learn Russian with a top-notch teacher. I was elated. To travel to Seltz! To be a young lady, a *panienke*, and go to the teacher with my books; to sleep in late and take walks with the big-city girls. . . . I created a whole new world in my head. I imagined what I would see in Seltz, and what it would be like afterward when I came back home. Everyone would ask me for the news from the city, and everyone would be jealous because I knew so much, and because I was so refined, and because I knew Russian. Perhaps I would even learn to read a Russian book. Who knew? My thoughts carried me farther and farther away. Once I could speak and read Russian, I would be able to chat with the Russian Orthodox priest's daughters, the *panienkes*. Perhaps I would even stay at the boardinghouse in

Seltz, together with all the rich girls. I would wear a brown school dress and go to class every day with my books. I quivered with joy when I thought about it all. I hoped against hope and waited, without understanding where such happiness could come from. I waited for a miracle, as if by chance I would be transported to Seltz.

I looked forward so eagerly to being transported to the city that I actually rejoiced on one occasion when lightning set fire to a gentile's cottage in our shtetl, and the blaze spread from there to an area with a lot of Jewish homes.

By the time the fire reached our house, everyone was weeping, but I was secretly delighted. I sat in the meadow behind the shtetl, surrounded by our pillows, bedding, clothes, jackets, brass candlesticks, and cooking pots. I kept watch over our belongings, while other girls also guarded their things nearby. The sky was red from the fire. The entire shtetl was engulfed in smoke; we couldn't see any of the houses. I could hear people running, and voices wailing, and children screaming. Meanwhile, I was thinking that our home must have already burned down, and I was hoping that now we would head off to Seltz, since what would we have left to do here, if our home had been reduced to ashes? We'd sell the lot, and with the proceeds, we'd open a store in the city. I figured we already had one foot in the door in Seltz.

But then my mother came running up with the joyful news that our home had remained intact. God had directed that not a single Jewish home should burn down, she said. I was not pleased with this news, but so be it; I kept that to myself and helped my mother bring our bundles back home. By nighttime we had put everything back in order, and we went back to being simple, small-shtetl people as before. At that point, I stopped hoping that we would ever live in a big city, but I consoled myself with my mother's promise to send me to Seltz for a couple of months to learn how to write Russian.

Unlucky child, your hopes are futile! Enough learning already! Prepare yourself to do something more important than studying. Other things are waiting for you: you will work, but even your work will be in vain. Death was once again thinking about how to visit our home, and it turns out that this time he thought about it for a long time before he decided to go in. For three years he sat there, whetting his sacrificial knife, and he kept trying it out on his unlucky victim to see if it was sharp.

It was the Seventeenth of Tammuz that summer—the commemoration of the day when the Romans first breached the walls of Jerusalem before the destruction of the Second Temple—when my mother began to cough for the first time in such a way that our own walls began to shake. This is when that terrible guest tried out his sacrificial knife for the first time, and the walls trembled at the injustice that Death wanted to deprive two small fatherless children of their mother as well.

My mother had felt unwell for weeks, but everyone figured it was because she had taken fright on the first day of Pesach. My mother was in shul when the priest's daughter, Sashke the *panienke*, suddenly burst in, yelling that our house was on fire. My mother ran out; it seemed from afar that our roof really was on fire, and she raised a cry. Everyone ran out of the synagogues and started carrying water over to our house, but when someone climbed up onto our roof, there was no sign of a blaze. No one could understand. A couple of dozen men and women stood around asking, what happened to the fire?

Sashke the *panienke* stood apart, laughing about how she had fooled a whole shtetl of Jews. None of the Jews had known about the custom that, on the first of April, people were supposed to play tricks on each other. She explained to my mother afterward that this was not an insult, that on this day it was fine to trick anybody, even the most important people. And thus did our shtetl discover that there is a day in this world called April Fools' Day. But this cost my mother very dearly—she got sick, and for an entire month afterward, she had to take my little brother and me to the *opshprekherin* to be treated for our fear.

I had been to the *opshprekherin* many times before, both to ward off the evil eye as well as to chase away my fears. Whenever my head hurt, my mother would take me off to Hinde Yuel, the top *opshprekherin* in our shtetl. I used to see her almost every week. She would sit on a large bench with her patient at her feet on a small stool. Her lips would quiver, but I never heard her speak any words. I had little faith in her mastery; I thought that she didn't know anything, which was why she only moved her lips and didn't speak aloud.

This was my impression for a long time, until one day I found an incantation to ward off the evil eye in one of my grandmother's prayer books. I saw then that I had sinned against Hinde the *opshprekherin*, because there really was an incantation against the evil eye, and probably, I told myself, you're supposed to recite it silently. I immediately learned the incantation from my grandmother's book, and as soon as my head started to hurt, I would recite it myself, as if it really were a cure.

That summer, when my mother had her fright, I was very weak and feverish. My face was as yellow as wax, which everyone said was because of my own fear. Our neighbor Basia-Reyzl told my mother that if she wanted me to get better, she should send me to the village of Kalatsia, to see Shumle the *opshprekher*. When Shumle worked his magic, she said, it cured his patients in no time. Meanwhile, I was delighted to be traveling to Kalatsia. This was no small thing, to travel over the river in a rowboat that would glide so beautifully through the water, and then to visit Kalatsia itself.

Kalatsia was a tiny hamlet not far from our shtetl. The only way to get there was by boating across the river, and not everyone could do this, since a lot of people were scared to travel by boat. We children longed to cross the river, but our parents wouldn't let us. The boys would steal off with friends anyway and boat over to Kalatsia. Who do boys listen to? Nothing is too hard for them. But we unfortunate girls, what could we do? If your mother says you can't go, then you don't go.

And so I was delighted when my mother said that I would go to Kalatsia that evening to be treated by Shumle. I spent the whole day thinking about how I would enjoy the trip. In the evening, I went off with Golda, the wife of the Kalatsia smith; my mother would not have entrusted me to anyone else. Golda used to come to the shtetl every day to buy goods in our store to take back to Kalatsia, because she didn't have the capital to buy enough to last for a few days. She had her own boat, which she rowed skillfully; it took her a total of five minutes to cross the river. At first, when I sat down in her boat and looked at the water, I was a bit afraid. The water seemed as dark as the clouds in the sky, and I worried about falling into the abyss. But when I looked at Golda's great big figure and her thick dark hands, and when I saw how nimble and quick she was with the oar, I laughed at myself for being afraid. I understood that traveling by boat with Golda was like walking over an iron bridge.

Night had fallen by the time Golda delivered me to Kalatsia. She brought me to Shimen the Hasid's home, explained to Shimen's wife why I had come, and then left. Shimen the Hasid's wife, Frume-Gita, was herself from our shtetl; her father was distantly related to our family. She welcomed me as an honored guest and treated me like a near relation. She put on the kettle and made me a cup of sweet tea, which I had with challah left over from Shabbes. She asked me what was the matter, and she questioned me about my mother and about what was happening in the shtetl. When I had given her all the details and had a rest, we went off to see Shumle the *opshprekher.*

Shumle was one of the richest gentiles in Kalatsia. He was respectable and dignified; that is, he lived in high style. He had a reputation for not drinking liquor, and it was said that this was the reason he was so wealthy. He also had a reputation as a healer, but he wouldn't accept much money for this; he was satisfied with the honor alone. He knew my mother well, because he often patronized her store, so she hadn't sent any money as payment; instead she sent a pound of sugar and half an ounce of tea, as a gift.

When I went inside Shumle's house, I was so surprised that I stood stock-still. This was the first time in my life I had been inside a gentile's home. I saw a room full of boys, girls, men, and women. They were all tall and healthy, with ruddy cheeks, and they were engrossed in their work: the girls and the women were weaving and spinning, and the boys were weaving fiber from bark to make the bast shoes that country Russians wore. Old Shumle himself sat on the ground, chopping kindling and feeding the fire. An old woman raked potatoes out of the hot oven into a bucket, and the whole family sat down to eat supper. The potatoes were set near the table with a large jug of cold cucumber brine, and two large loaves of bread were laid on the table. The gentiles gobbled everything up in five minutes flat. When they were finished eating, they immediately sat back down to their work, and they weren't sad or depressed about it; they were happy, and they sang together in a beautiful chorus of mixed voices. Meanwhile Shumle sat himself down in a little corner with me and quietly spoke his spells. Frume-Gita passed the time with the old woman, who was now splitting the kindling and lighting it. I looked at them all and realized that I had unjustifiably thought that the gentiles lived poorly, because they were always toiling, and they lived in tiny, smoky cottages, and they ate simple food. I had always thought that the simple gentiles were the unluckiest people on earth. But now, sitting with Shumle in his home, I saw that I had made a huge mistake. Before my own eyes was the cottage with its burning kindling and the happy, healthy faces of people who were sitting and singing while they worked. For the first time, I understood how Shumle could be happy with his life of peaceful work.

Shumle finished his incantations and gave me a flask of yellow liquid to drink. I accepted it together with his thanks for my mother's present and went away with Frume-Gita. I spent the night at Frume-Gita's and slept very well.

Golda came at daybreak and woke me up to take me home. I dressed quickly, said goodbye to Frume-Gita and her daughters, and went with Golda to the riverbank. When we got in the boat, the sun had just started to rise, but it was hidden behind the barns and we couldn't see it. The sky was blue; the river was perfectly calm and silent. I listened to the slap of the oar on the water while I let my mind wander, thinking how beautiful it was. Suddenly I saw a flash of fire. The whole river was emblazoned with blue, and the water began to shimmer with all kinds of colors. My eyes ached, looking at all the stunning colors, among which the blue, gold and red stood out most of all. When I had gotten my fill of looking at the water, I lifted my eyes. I saw that the sun had just then risen above the barns. We were already coming to the other side of the river and had almost reached the bank. Reluctantly I got out of the rowboat and walked home distractedly. When I got home, I ran into the garden, and there I silently cried myself out, not knowing why. My head hurt the entire day, probably because I had gotten up so early. But in any case, Shumle's healing helped, and I started to feel better. My little brother also drank the yellow liquid that Shumle had given me, and it helped him as well.

My brother and I had nearly forgotten about the fright we had had on April Fools' Day, but my mother grew weaker and weaker. She caught a cold on the way home from Seltz and developed a severe cough. Bit by bit, she began to lose her appetite as well. When she went to Seltz for merchandise, her friends told her to go see a doctor. But she countered that she had no time to busy herself with that; so long as the children were healthy, thank God, that was good enough for her.

A few weeks passed, and my mother got progressively worse. It finally got so bad by erev Rosh Hashanah that she went to the doctor in Seltz. From there, she went to Senziv to a more famous doctor. The doctors declared that her illness was a catarrh of the lungs, a chronic inflammation that could last for many years. They also said with this kind of illness, it was best for the patient to have a rich purse and a couple of healthy people who could look after her.

6

Seltz

My mother settled in Seltz, surrounded by little flasks and boxes of medications. Every day another doctor came and prescribed something different. She choked down all the bitter preparations, but none of them helped; day by day, she went from bad to worse. One doctor gave her medicine to suppress her cough, but then my poor mother became so congested, she could hardly breathe. A second doctor then gave her something to encourage her to cough, so she could breathe more easily, but this made her cough so hard she felt as if her sides would burst, and they ached with pain. Yet a third doctor came and put cupping glasses all over her with a blistering agent made of Spanish flies, which covered her entire body in open sores. Finally she screamed that the doctors were killing her, that she hadn't felt this bad when she first came to see them. All three of the doctors gathered for a consultation and decided that their flasks and boxes of medicines weren't doing any good. She didn't need any prescriptions; all she needed was fresh air, good food, lots of rest, and not to worry about anything.

Every day, one of the doctors would come check on her. This is how they left it.

My mother saw that her illness was going to drag on for some time. She didn't want to be so far from home by herself, so she wrote a plaintive letter to my grandmother in Rishelevsk, saying that at thirty-eight years old, she needed a nanny. And, as she wrote, who would be better than her own mother?

In the meantime, she was in good hands; she was staying with an old friend, the dear, devout Ester-Musha, who had no children and was therefore always looking to perform mitzvahs. I was home then, and I didn't know about any of this. My mother wrote me letters, but she didn't tell me how badly she was doing. She just wrote that she wasn't sparing any expense and was being tended to by the best doctors, who were visiting her three times a day and occasionally at night too. I didn't understand what these frequent visits meant. I thought it was good the doctors were coming so often; I figured the more they came, the sooner she would get better.

At the time, I looked on doctors as some kind of special, superior beings, so I was not terribly frightened by my mother's illness. I believed the doctors would soon cure her: they were agents of God. It simply couldn't be otherwise. I just prayed for it to happen quickly, since God and everyone else could see how I was suffering without my mother. I was only twelve years old. Not long before, I hadn't known how to do anything; now I had to run the store and take care of the home too. But this was probably meant to be my destiny.

My hope was that by fall, my mother would be healthy and return home for Sukkos, and in those happier times, we would finally be able to tell each other everything we had been through. Until then, I prepared for the holidays as always, since my mother had written that I shouldn't spoil our celebrations. On Rosh Hashanah, I went to shul to hear the shofar. When I went to the seat my mother had rented, over by the eastern wall, I found someone sitting in her spot. This felt like a stab to my heart. The woman immediately gave me the seat, but she looked at me with pity and said, "Pray to God for your mother to be cured, my child!" Her words hit me like a hammer. I didn't want her pity, and I was furious that she had told me to pray for my mother's health. What did she mean? Did I not already know I should pray to God? When I looked around, it turned out that all the women were giving me the same pitying looks. I grew even angrier and was careful not to look any of them in the eye. I sat down and studied a prayer with great intention.

I prayed very earnestly on both days of Rosh Hashanah, and after Rosh Hashanah, I fasted for a day. I did this all with God in mind, so he would send my mother a cure. Erev Yom Kippur, Khatzkel the coachman brought a letter from my mother, but it was not at all cheerful. She wrote that she was just as sick as she had been earlier, and she suffered terrible pains.

Meanwhile, the doctors had not helped at all, though they continued to give her hope. For now, it was not good, but she told us not to be afraid. "God will help us, children!" she wrote. "And you, my daughter," she added, "take care of the house, and be responsible in the store. Don't forget that I am counting on you for everything."

After we read my mother's letter, my little brother and I both had a good cry, and we decided to go visit her during the middle working days of Sukkos. With this in mind, I calmed down a bit. But that evening, while saying the blessing over the lighting of the candles, I heard our boarder Basia-Reyzl crying while she said the blessing in her room. She usually prayed on behalf of herself and her husband and their children. But now I heard her entreating God on behalf of my mother. It was then that I realized the truth about the danger my mother was in. Basia-Reyzl spoke to God about my mother's situation. She mentioned me and my brother and asked God not to leave us as true orphans. I listened to all of this silently, but hearing my name and "true orphan," I ran in to her in tears and begged her to tell me if my mother was still alive. She realized that I had overheard her and that I understood at last. Of course she reassured me as best as she could, and then she left for shul. I set myself to saying *Maariv,* the evening prayers, not so much with a cry as with a scream. I didn't notice the gentile girls standing outside my window, laughing at how I had gone crazy. They told me later that I was rolling

around on the ground, that I ripped the hair out of
my head and tore an apron to pieces, forgetting that
by now it was Yom Kippur, when it was forbidden to
tear anything or do any work. (For this transgression,
I fasted an additional day, and I still figured that God
had not forgiven me.)

I carried on like this until after shul, when a few
dozen people came and consoled me and got me to
stop screaming. They told me to ignore Basia-Reyzl's
babbling; I would do better to listen to what the
coachman Khatzkel the Tall had said. Khatzkel had
seen my mother himself, and he had heard the doctor say that she would be healthy again in another
month. This calmed me down, and I stopped crying.
My little brother, who had also cried himself out, had
fallen asleep. The women dispersed quietly until only
Basia-Reyzl remained, dozing next to me on a chair.
The regular candles had burned down, but an enormous wax candle stood burning in a metal pitcher
filled with sand. The shadows from our four candlesticks splayed out eerily on the wall. Our mirror,
which hung on the wall and was cracked in several
places, was especially dreadful; I saw a different picture in each of its fragments. In one, it seemed that
I saw my mother, dressed in white. I was frightened
out of my wits, quickly covered my head, and started
reciting the *Shema*. But I fell asleep while I was saying
it, with the sweet sleep of a twelve-year-old child.

The next morning, I woke up late. Everyone was
already in shul, even my little brother. I quickly got up

and began praying; I was already much calmer than the day before. When I finished praying, I began to reflect about the situation, and after a couple of hours, I realized that it was completely ridiculous for me to have cried so much that my head still hurt today. How could my mother not recover? She was still young, and had she sinned in some way against God? Not at all; she was so devout. It simply could not be! God would hear our prayers, I became resolved, and my mother would recover. We had so many people to pray for her: my grandmother alone could split all seven layers of heaven with her prayers; in addition, there was me, my brother, my aunt Zlata, my aunt Beyle, my aunt Tobe, Basia-Reyzl, even strangers—the entire shtetl was praying for my mother. Aside from them, we had many intercessors in the world to come who could plead on her behalf: my father himself, who had been a great *tsaddik*, would of course intercede, and his entreaty would certainly carry weight. And what about my mother's grandfathers and grandmothers? The living and the dead would unite in advocating for her recovery. "Oh, my mother *will* get better!" I cried out, and I set myself to reciting psalms.

On Sukkos, I received a letter from my mother that she was doing better, and that we shouldn't come to visit, because the store shouldn't be left alone. I cheered up at the news and I thought, God really did hear our prayers. Thank you, God, for your mercy!

After Sukkos, I had to travel to Seltz for merchandise, so I finally got to go see my mother. My mother's youngest sister Tsipe, who lived in a nearby village, traveled with me.

Traveling to Seltz after Sukkos was no easy task, because fall was the muddiest time of the year. Three coachmen traveled to Seltz from our shtetl every week: Khatzkel the Tall, Itse son of Motl, and Fayvke with the white horse, or Fayvke the Shlimazel, as he was called. Fayvke got that name because he was very poor. He lived in a rickety cottage, which was all that he owned. Even the white horse didn't belong to him, since he owed more on it than the horse was worth. But God had lavished blessings on Fayvke in one respect—he didn't skimp on giving him children. Fayvke was already on his third wife and had children from all of them; he must have had a full dozen. God gave him his all with the children, though, since Fayvke did not have the smallest bit of luck in any other regard.

Fayvke would travel to Seltz just like the other coachmen, but the others would profit from their trips, and he would not—somehow, by the time he returned home, none of his earnings would be left. This was because Fayvke was incredibly lazy. He used to leave on a Sunday, and he would hole himself up at Bere the cantor's place in Seltz for the entire week. During the same period, the other coachmen would make the trip three times. Meanwhile, his horse would eat up the small profit he had earned, and there was nothing left for his wife and children. Fayvke's wife, Perl, managed to prepare a nice Shabbes anyway, poor thing. She endured, and she borrowed, promising to pay everyone back right away when her husband came the following day. But when her husband finally did show up, all he said was that they needed to borrow a sack of oats for the horse for Shabbes; that was the sum total of his earnings for the week. People wondered how they lived. But Perl was a very efficient housewife, and she knew how to make things easier and how to brighten their lives.

Despite his poverty, Fayvke was always merry. He seemed happier than the wealthiest man in the shtetl, Aharon Rokhes, who was always distracted and worried about his business. Fayvke never worried about anything; he always looked content.

Our second coachman was Itse son of Motl. Itse was a completely different kind of man, also cheerful, but somewhat quick-tempered, and not at all lazy. All the passengers respected him, whereas they made fun of Fayvke. Itse didn't stand on ceremony with anyone and spoke his mind, even to people with the highest standing. He also didn't chase after his livelihood. He held respectability in greater esteem than money, so in the absence of high-class passengers, he preferred to stay home, especially since he didn't need much to live on. His brother always said that Itse and his wife Rasha could live a whole week just fine on a pot of barley and two calves' feet.

In comparison with the others, our third coachman was a member of the aristocracy: this was Khatzkel the Tall, the husband of the talented Khaye-Beyla.

Khatzkel was yet another kind of person, neither merry nor quick-tempered, but an unpleasant, hugely arrogant man. His arrogance set in, people said, after he married Khaye-Beyla.

Our shtetl was oppressed by these three coachmen. We shopkeepers felt it most, since we used their services so often, but anyone who rode with them really suffered. They squeezed their coaches so full of passengers we could hardly breathe; in the end, we couldn't feel our arms or legs, and everyone would be dead tired. We would leave our shtetl in the evening and arrive at our first stop at Mote's inn in Suretse at midnight, to tend to the horses. The coachman unhitched the horses, and we made ourselves at home; everyone sat around the table with tea from the samovar and two strings of bagels for supper. Supper lasted a full three hours, because it wasn't a silent affair: people told stories about everything from thieves and horses and coachmen to Orthodox rabbis and Hasidic rebbes and ritual slaughterers, and everyone had a joke to share. We spent a few hours there, then piled back into the coach and traveled on until morning. In the morning, we arrived at our next rest stop, in Kliv. This was a tavern in the middle of a field, not far from Seltz. We stopped and everyone prayed, ate breakfast, spent a bit of time with the people in the tavern— there must have been a hundred people there—and then crammed ourselves back into the coach. We arrived in Seltz at eleven o'clock in the morning. And so it would take fourteen hours to travel six miles, and by the time we got to Bere the cantor's in Seltz, I couldn't even straighten out my legs. We could rest completely at Bere's, though, and Bere and his family were such dear people that they didn't accept any money; this was a kind of charity for them. Fayvke made himself comfortable there for an entire week.

However unpleasant the journey was, I had always enjoyed it during the good times, because I was so glad to go to the city. Now when I was traveling to see my sick mother, I was completely exasperated by the trip. But just as all things pass, I made it through that too.

I could hardly wait to see my mother, but first, a surprise: my grandmother had arrived just a couple of hours earlier from Rishelevsk. My grandmother Feyga from so far away—this was no small thing! Whenever she visited, it felt like a holiday. Even though she scolded us constantly, we didn't mind, because she would bring such a great assortment of things from all over.

Now, as I looked at my mother, I realized that this holiday would not be as joyful as usual. My grandmother had indeed brought nice things, but they were of no interest to me. I only had eyes for my mother, who looked dreadful, and almost not human: her face was yellow, her lips white, her eyes nearly extinguished, her chest sunken, and her arms emaciated—what had happened to my beautiful mother?! I consoled myself when my mother said that she was doing better, and we could hope to God that she would quickly return to normal. At this, everyone cheered up except my grandmother; her ancient, practical eye had taken in my mother's appearance, and she understood how my mother was really doing. Since my grandmother had little faith in my mother's improvement, she began contemplating what to do, and she decided that first off, we should go to the cemetery and remind our ancestors not to forget about us.

"We need to remind them whose life is at stake," my grandmother told me. "Thank God, there are those in the world to come who know your mother! She has plenty of relatives who can advocate for her there." My mother had been very dear to her grandfather and her grandmother, and her aunt Kreyne, who had helped my grandmother raise her children, would definitely not remain silent; she would smash through any barriers and go straight to God's throne to ask him to spare the life of this young woman, this beautiful widow, this mother of small children. Oh, none of them would remain silent! "And it's not just anybody who will advocate for her," my grandmother added, "but *tsaddikim*, whose prayers have real worth. But they need to be reminded."

My mother's friend Ester-Musha had already been to the cemetery to appeal to the dead, together with Rivke the *zogerin*, the women's prayer leader and professional mourner. Rivke could successfully importune the most hardhearted of souls with her prayers, so she would certainly prevail with those who were not so callous. "But it's not enough for strangers to go," my grandmother said. "The dead love to be respected, and we ourselves must visit them. You come too, my daughter," she told me, "You can shed a few tears on your father's grave too and entreat him to intercede for your mother, so that God will grant her health."

I listened to her carefully and determined not to forget what I was supposed to say to my father. But I wasn't able to think for long, because we left right away for the cemetery: me, my grandmother, my aunt Zlata, and my aunt Tsipe. Ester-Musha said that we should bring along Rivke the *zogerin* as well, because it would be unbecoming to go without her, but my grandmother scoffed at the idea. "What do you mean?" she said. "Are we some kind of public bath attendants? We don't know Hebrew? We can read the *Mayne-loshn* as well as the *zogerins*." The *Mayne-loshn*, I knew, was the book of prayers one said in a cemetery. "So what do we need her for?"

And truth be told, we did not dishonor ourselves on those worthy premises. As soon as we arrived, the caretakers recognized that we were not simple women, since every one of us held our own *Mayne-loshn*, and they could see we were well educated. But they were even more impressed when we told them whose graves we were there to see, because we were going to visit such eminent people. My father's name had the strongest effect on them, and we went to visit him first. Even though some of our other intercessors were older than my father, his reputation surpassed them all.

I had never been to my father's grave, and I could hardly wait; I expected something wondrous to behold. I walked on, reading the names on the graves. At last we stopped by a simple wooden marker where my father's eminent name shone out, along with all his honorifics, which were so numerous they completely filled the board. As I slowly read through the descriptions, I thought what a great man my father had been. All of my father's titles, and those of his grandfathers, I took onto myself, and a shiver of pride passed through my bones. My head lifted as if I were exalted, and I stood like a true princess.

I compared my father's gravestone to those of strangers. On the others were written only a few cold words, while on my father's, I read: *Son of the rabbi, the eminent Talmudist, the* tsaddik, *the prominent scholar, the glory of Israel,* and on, and on . . . I was so absorbed with my father's considerable reputation that I completely forgot what was happening around me, and why I had come. I would have stood engrossed in my thoughts even longer, but my grandmother yanked my arm; why was I standing there so distracted? When I looked up, I saw that my grandmother and my aunts had tears flowing down their cheeks. They weren't even reading the *Mayne-loshn*, but the words that came out of their mouths could have come straight from it. They spoke as fluently as if they were reading from a prayer book; even stones could have been moved by their lamentations.

I was jealous that they could speak so well. I wanted to say something too, but I didn't know where to begin. I began to read from the *Mayne-loshn*, but it sounded ridiculous; I sounded like someone who was reading the Haggadah at a joyful Passover seder, and I wouldn't be able to cry unless I started hitting myself. I was beside myself and thoroughly ashamed; my grandmother and my aunts would certainly think I was a complete fool for not understanding that I was supposed to weep. But what could I do? I wanted to cry, but no tears came, and to present arguments like theirs was something I also couldn't do. I didn't know what to do, and I could hardly wait for them to move on from my father's grave.

I did not go to the rest of the graves. I sat indoors with the gravedigger until they came to get me. I had to wait a good bit, since they spent some time at the other graves importuning the dead and persuading them what needed to be done. Since my father was a man, and especially such a great man, they couldn't really admonish him, or complain to him like they wanted. But over at my great-grandmother's grave, and at my great-aunt Kreyne's—there, they could finally let loose. These were not just compassionate and pious people, but they were women. With them, it was easier to feel a connection; they spoke the same language. They too had been unhappy mothers with sick children, so they could sympathize. And of course, we had come to plead on behalf of their favorite child. My great-grandmother and my great-aunt Kreyne would surely remember how hard it had been when my mother grew up; they had stayed up many nights and endured many fasts to nurse her through all her childhood illnesses. They were barely able to raise her. And she was so beautiful, talented, and smart!

"But does she deserve a premature end, mother-in-law, like the rebel Korakh?" my grandmother screamed. "Why should such a young tree be torn down? You must not remain silent. May your merits protect her!" My grandmother rapped on the gravestone so my great-grandmother would listen. My mother was just as dear to the dead as she was to the living, but the dead knew better what to do. Now that my great-grandmother was a holy soul, she could reach places where the living could not go, and pray for her there. . . . So if she could help, she simply must!

It was already quite late when my grandmother and my aunts finished their visits at the cemetery. We couldn't walk back, because we all had fasted and they were exhausted from crying, so we took a droshky. My grandmother felt very unwell during the ride, but I knew this was not from fasting. There was nothing new about fasting for her. She almost always fasted on Mondays and Thursdays, as did many pious Jews. She fasted on the Ten Days of Repentance between Rosh Hashanah and Yom Kippur, and aside from these, on the other fast days throughout the year.

And then there were the vows and fasts that arose on ordinary days. If it happened that you didn't have enough time to pray, then you could find yourself at two o'clock without having eaten; by that time, it was hardly worth it, since it would soon be night and time to break fast. By my reckoning, my grandmother fasted three days a week, and the remaining days, it was the same to her if she ate or didn't. Whenever she had the chance to starve herself a bit, so much the better—any opportunity to torment her body. So what if she had eaten a good meal instead? There would just be a bit more flesh for the worms in her grave! In our foolish world, these things just don't matter. This is what my grandmother used to say, when her children begged her not to mortify herself.

So I understood that, when my grandmother's head hurt as we left the cemetery, it was not because she had fasted. She had bigger concerns. She had seen her ailing daughter with her own two eyes.

When we returned to my mother's, my grandmother went in with a cheerful expression and told her that now she would certainly get better: we had importuned everyone thoroughly, so they would act as good intercessors for her. My mother smiled at this, and everyone was happy to see it. We all believed that the good times would now begin. My mother asked how I had behaved at the cemetery: had I wept, had I not said anything foolish? She did not receive a suitable answer to these questions, however. She was only told that, for somebody my age, I had cried enough.

My mother was not pleased with this answer. What does it mean, for somebody her age? Her daughter should be a complete person at twelve years old. But what could one do? Such was her luck! She made no further comment.

It began to grow dark. The women said *Mincha*, the afternoon prayer, and we ate supper. Afterward, we all sat around my mother's bed, and my grandmother began to tell us her news. And she really had something to tell: she had just returned from the land of Israel. She had gone to visit her son, who was employed there in agriculture, just like the simple gentiles here at home. She had spent the entire summer there and traveled throughout the Holy Land. From Rishelevsk, she had traveled ten days by sea to Jaffa, then she rode on a donkey for four days to get to her son in his colony. My grandmother said he couldn't be happier, precisely because he was living in the Holy Land. Afterward, she went to see all the holy gravesites, and she went to Jerusalem and prayed at the Western Wall. My aunts were salivating to hear this, and tears flowed down their cheeks, they were so envious. They were especially moved to hear that she had visited the town of Tiberias, where the famous Reb Meir Baal HaNes lay buried, the ancient "Master of Miracles" who was so well known to all women. My aunts recalled how their hands trembled with awe whenever they simply went up to his alms box at shul, so to be by his gravesite—one could imagine how frightening it would be!

Then my grandmother told us about her visit to Rachel's Tomb. There is a shul at the site, she said, which the great philanthropist Sir Moses Montefiore had built, where all the travelers go to pray. And on the site grows a special kind of herb that helps heal all kinds of diseases. "I picked a sack of this herb," my grandmother told my mother, "and now it will be of good use for you, my daughter." She continued, "And moreover, I have another present for you: I went to visit the tomb of Reb Shimon bar Yochai, the Mishnaic sage. A Ner Tamid burns there, an Eternal Light. They pour fresh oil into it every month, and the oil that is left over from the previous month is treasured for its medicinal properties and allocated to the sick. As soon as they rub it on themselves, their disease is cured in no time at all. This oil is so treasured that even the Turks use it."

My mother had sat pensively the whole time without interrupting, but when she heard the name of Reb Shimon bar Yochai, she gave a start and cried, "Mama, what are you saying? I know that name very well. At home, the cabinets are filled with texts that speak of him!" And my mother fell silent and began to weep quietly, but in a way that pierced my heart. When she calmed down, she asked my grandmother to rub the oil on her. My grandmother did so, and my mother soon fell asleep with the precious, tranquil slumber of a healthy person. Of course she could sleep peacefully now, I thought, since Reb Shimon bar Yochai was also an intercessor for her, and he would meet with my father in the world to come as with a close acquaintance, and both of them would go straight to God's divine throne and pray for my mother. With these hopes, I fell asleep even more peacefully than my mother, and I dreamed that I saw my father with Reb Shimon bar Yochai, sitting next to a golden table in Paradise, and Paradise looked just the same as I had read about in the *Shevet Musar*.

In the morning, I asked my mother why she had cried when she heard the name of Reb Shimon bar Yochai. She answered that she had been thinking about my father and how engrossed he had been in the *Zohar*, which was thought to be his teachings. Reb Shimon bar Yochai's name was familiar to her because she had felt his spirit in her home for so many years.

That morning, my mother was a little happier than she had been the day before. This was already enough to make me feel happy too. My grandmother had been up all night with my aunt Zlata and my aunt Tsipe, telling them about the Holy Land, which had gotten them so excited they could not tear themselves away. I was really disappointed that I had fallen asleep. I wanted to hear all the stories too, but my grandmother promised to tell me everything separately. My aunts said goodbye, heaped blessings on my mother, and left for home. I left to go around the city to buy merchandise to bring home. My mother gave me a note to take to each shopkeeper, in which she asked them not to inflate the prices for me. The notes really made an impression on them. I bought the best merchandise, and I was treated with respect everywhere I went. Everyone asked how old I was; they praised me and said that I was smart, and I was in seventh heaven. I was very pleased with myself that day.

In the evening, I left for home, and my grandmother remained with my mother in Seltz. The doctors had said that after a couple of weeks, she would be able to go home, but that she would have to be looked after very carefully. She had to be in a room with high ceilings and a dry whitewashed floor, without any dust; the windows should be open so fresh air could come in, even in the middle of winter, and then the room should be heated so that it was warm. And they ordered a thousand equally ridiculous things. I couldn't understand this at all: what did they mean, first cool down the room completely, and then warm it up, and on the next day cool it down and then warm it up again? What was the point? But if a doctor said to do it, he probably knew.

I hired Reyze the water carrier to help me get the house ready for my mother. She did the whitewashing, and we both cleaned everything as if it were Pesach. Every day I opened the windows and then heated the space, just as the doctor had ordered. No one was allowed in the room, not even my little brother, but before bed, we would both go look at how bright and beautiful it was and imagine how happy our mother would be there. Once, before we went to sleep, when

I asked my little brother what he was thinking, he said that he was thinking how he would enjoy living in such a room. I replied that I myself had seen people living in even more beautiful rooms.

"Where did you see that?" he asked me.

"In Seltz, at the home of Kozlovsky the doctor."

"Oh, at a doctor's!" he scoffed. "But have you ever seen a home like that for ordinary people?"

"I don't know about ordinary people," I answered.

And every evening we had a little chat like this about how nice the room was.

7

Things Deteriorate

The weeks passed, and my mother arrived home
with my grandmother on a cold, bright Thursday.
I unlocked the "Passover chamber," as my brother
called the room I had prepared for my mother; she
inspected it and was pleased. An entire pharmacy of
flasks and boxes of medicine was carried in, and visitors began to arrive soon afterward. Everyone made
a fuss: my mother had come! They all wanted to see
her—our neighbors, our relatives, and the shtetl's
finest residents. Our neighbor Khaye-Ita, her aunt
Malke-Rokhl, and Khaye-Beyla were the first to arrive. Khaye-Ita and her aunt were overcome with joy.
They asked my mother countless questions, waited on
her, and gave her their best wishes. Then my aunts
and cousins arrived, and the wealthiest woman in
the shtetl, Aharon-Rokhes's wife Golda-Leah, and
Leybe the cantor with Mendl Karovitser. My grandmother then closed the door and refused to let anyone
else in. Nonetheless, those few people tracked in so
much snow that you could slide across the floor of the
Passover chamber, because in those days, no one was

wearing galoshes yet. The room got so chilly with all the snow that my mother had to wrap herself in a warm shawl.

The visitors pelted my mother with questions. If her cough prevented her from answering, they kept repeating the question until she could speak, and everyone kept talking and talking. My grandmother realized that things were getting out of hand—no one was even thinking about leaving, and my mother's lips were already dry from talking—so she began to ask people discreetly to go home. One by one they began to depart. It came off well; my mother didn't notice my grandmother asking people to go. She also didn't ask anyone to stay; she simply asked them to come visit her often. Leybe the cantor, a spirited and merry man, replied that he would definitely not be back, because she was no longer as beautiful as she used to be. Everyone burst out laughing. There was nothing new about Leybe's joking; he had quite a reputation for his wit.

Leybe the cantor was a tall, thin man with dark, blazing eyes and a waxy yellow face. He had ten or so children of all sizes, large and small, and he was perpetually poor; he worried constantly about his livelihood. His second wife was a short, dark woman, with a sallow face like her husband's. Both of them were always sick. She had a lung disease, and when she had to draw a deep breath, she would close her eyes in pain. He had some kind of inflammation of his throat and nose, and he spoke in a hoarse voice. He was always loafing about, roaming from one house to another, crying that he was on the verge of dying, his throat was choking him, and he would soon suffocate . . . and then he would tell such a funny joke that everyone was rolling in laughter. Everyone laughed about his illness; no one believed he was serious. He visited us frequently and talked about his troubles. He went around like this for a good many years. Then one bright, beautiful day, when he went to my aunt Zlata's store and began telling jokes as always, he began to wheeze, his eyes suddenly rolled back in his head, and he collapsed on the ground. Everyone was shocked. At first, people thought he was feigning, but then they could see he was not moving, and someone ran to fetch Khone the healer. Khone came right away, but by then, Leybe was lying dead on my aunt Zlata's sofa. Someone said that he should be bled, but this didn't help; they nicked his skin and placed cupping glasses on his body, but no blood flowed.

People thronged around to see how Leybe the cantor had finally died for real. His wife and children soon came running too. As was the custom, she began wailing and the other women did as well, but she couldn't speak a single word. She was soon out of breath, and Khone the healer set about trying to revive her on the other sofa. The scene at my aunt Zlata's was just indescribable. Before long, the shammes arrived from the shul, and he hired Fayvke the coachman to take Leybe away to Seltz, since we didn't yet have a cemetery of our own in the shtetl. The following morning, my aunt Zlata baked a couple dozen loaves of bread for the widow and her children, and the next week, someone else did the same. A couple of months passed this way, until Leybe the cantor's wife lost all her strength, struggling to breathe, and one morning, she simply didn't wake up. Fayvke the coachman took her away just he had earlier taken her husband, and their young children were sent somewhere to live with their older siblings. And what became of them, no one knows even today, because who was left to be interested?

Everyone remembers Leybe the cantor well. To this day, the shtetl still hasn't been able to find a cantor who is a good fit, not because everyone is so musical, but because everyone was so used to the way Leybe prayed. After all, he was our cantor for fifteen years! And his cheerfulness, and his witticisms . . . he is missed at every wedding, every bris, and every celebration of the birth of a son. There's not one holiday or Shabbes, no joyful evening in the shtetl, where Leybe isn't remembered.

Mendl Karovitser was quite a character too, but he was a simple man, not a cantor, so he didn't go visiting from house to house as Leybe did. Mendl was a bent-over, cheerful little old man. I never knew what his livelihood had been in his youth, but he had been involved in some kind of trade in the nearby villages; in his old age, he lived with a son. They never had enough bread to fill their stomachs; his wife and children were always hungry, except for Shabbes and holidays, and no one knew how he managed to get food then either. Mendl said that God helped him, but no one understood how God did so. He had even been a craftsman—he was a good bookbinder—but he never had any work, because everyone's books were already bound. Mendl mourned my father deeply, since my father had often given him work; after my father had died, no scholars had replaced him, so there was no one left to buy books. My father had been a great lover of all kinds of books. He bought not only old books, but also new ones, which he would get bound right away. My mother always complained that she could never settle up with the bookbinder, but in any case, Mendl's children had something to eat, though my mother might have had to do without. Anyway, Mendl was still alive, content, and witty. He had a story for every occasion and a parable for every situation. He would tell his stories in the study hall, while sitting by the great heating oven where he used to nap, or at our store when it was crowded with women, or on the porch at my aunt Zlata's, where young people would pass the time with her son. Such beautiful stories he told: they were simple, but they made an impression. Everyone stopped and listened when he began to speak; they drank in his words. Even the young scamps and rascals in the study hall would grow serious when he started telling a story; they would sit down quietly, like kittens, and listen to every word. None of his stories ever fell flat. I wonder where he got them from?

I always wanted to remember Mendl's stories so I could tell them again just like he did, but I've forgotten them all, except for one about the mitzvah of honoring your parents. Notah the ritual slaughterer once told Mendl about how fortunate he was in his son, who honored him with such respect. On hearing this, Mendl replied that this was no great thing; he had seen sons even better than Notah's. One time, he related, he was traveling to Zamir, and he stopped off at a village for Shabbes. He went to the inn and asked the innkeeper, a man of fifty, if he could celebrate Shabbes there. The innkeeper answered that he didn't know; he would have to ask his father, and he immediately shouted out, "Papa!" Mendl cracked a smile that a man of fifty couldn't commit himself without checking with his father. Soon there emerged a man of sixty-five and asked what they needed him for, and when he was told, he answered just as his son had done: he didn't know; he would have to ask his father, and he too cried out, "Papa!" Mendl shrugged his shoulders and wondered how long this was going to go on; they could keep this up until they got all the way back to Adam. Soon there emerged a bent old man of eighty years. His son and his grandson explained to him why they had called him, and he immediately nodded his head, that Mendl could spend Shabbes with them, and he went away. Mendl spent a very fine Shabbes there. The table was prepared beautifully. A couple dozen people sat around the table; these were children from four generations of the family. The little old man recited the kiddush over a great cup that held a full quart of wine, and everyone answered "Amen" very loudly; then everyone drank a sip from the cup, one after the other, and the old man took a little wine away into the second room. He did the same with every dish during the entire Shabbes. Mendl couldn't figure out who was there in the second room. He could hardly wait for havdalah, at the close of Shabbes, to ask the old man to whom he was taking the food. The old man did not answer, but beckoned for Mendl to follow him, and he led him into the second room, where he pointed out two tiny little people who were sitting in a corner, amusing themselves like small children. By their gray heads, one could see that these were the old man's father and mother, and their son had been bringing them their food. Now that is what's known as honoring your parents!

Mendl Karovitser, and earlier Leybe the cantor, came by often to visit my mother, and their stories really helped. She grew calmer and happier, and she ate better. My grandmother asked them to come as often as possible.

My mother's health improved somewhat, and one day she felt well enough to come to the store to help me out a bit. But before long, Stepan the drunkard came in, and he left the door open behind him. A wet wind and a cold rain followed him in and hit my mother full in the face; she had a coughing fit and had to go back to her room. She caught a bad cold and

could not get rid of her cough. A doctor came in from
Seltz to see her, but all he said was that she needed to
be careful, and now even more so, and with that he
went away.

After my mother caught her cold, a rough period began for my grandmother and me. My mother
coughed all night long; it was terrible to see her suffering. My grandmother and I would alternate sitting up with her: I one night, and she the next. It
was worse for my grandmother, since she would finish off my nights too, because around four o'clock I
would fall over like a stone—I simply couldn't stay
awake any longer. I tried all kinds of strategies to
avoid falling asleep. I lay on bare boards without a
pillow, and I splashed clean water on my eyes every
hour. But nothing helped; my eyes stuck together all
the same. Once, seeing me sitting there, my mother
dissolved into tears and told me to lie down. I obeyed
straight away and it took no more than two minutes
for me to fall into a deep sleep, not even noticing the
bare boards or my fist under my head instead of a pillow. But I wasn't asleep more than ten minutes when
I heard my mother cry out. She shook me awake and
spoke to me, first with kindness and then in anger.
Even though I heard her, I was not able to open my
eyes. Finally I managed to pry them open and ask her
why she was crying. She answered that she felt sick,
she couldn't catch her breath, and she was afraid to
be alone. And she was upset because she had a daughter like me, who didn't feel any compassion for her

and who left her all alone. "Raising children!" she said. "How much I endured for you, bringing you up; how many nights I stayed awake, and this is how you repay me!"

I sat and looked at her, not knowing what to say; I knew that she was right. I glanced at the clock: it was only half past one, and my eyes refused to stay open. A punishment from God! What could I do? My mother told me to lie down and sleep again, since she couldn't bear to see me suffer, but I managed to stay awake until my grandmother got up. Things went on like this for a month, and I kept looking for ways to drive away the sleep. In the end, I stumbled on a method. One night I was sitting with my mother, and the sound of her coughing resounded from the rafters. I counted every cough, thinking each one would finally be the last, but every time, another cough would come. This went on for a couple of hours. My mother's face had turned blue. Watching her and listening to her cough, my heart began to hurt so much that I felt pushed to my limit, and I squeezed one hand in the other and pinched it so hard that I felt it start to bleed. I began tearing little pieces of flesh from my hands. It hurt a good bit, but it kept me from falling asleep.

The nights dragged on endlessly. It was such a contrast to the days when my mother had been well, when the nights had flown past, and there was never enough time to sleep oneself out. My mother especially loved Shabbes nights in the winter. She would go to bed at seven in the evening and get up at seven in the morning; she slept a full twelve hours. And Shabbes itself had a completely different flavor when my mother had been well; we all felt it. When my mother got up on those mornings, she would announce: "Woe to the unbelievers who don't observe Shabbes, this dear, holy day!" Now it just wasn't the same, even though we would by no means profane the day; despite the fact that there was a serious illness in the house, my mother would have died rather than eat a meal cooked fresh on Shabbes. But there was simply nothing to be cheerful about now. My grandmother and I prayed and read all day just as we used to; women gathered at our home just as they always had; we had baked just as much challah—everything was just as it had been, but still, Shabbes was somehow different. With my mother sick, all the joy and pleasure were gone from the day.

After Chanukah, my grandmother left to go back home to Rishelevsk, and I took over her duties as well. I sat up every night that winter, leaning against a pillow and tearing larger and larger pieces of flesh from my hands; I went around with open wounds on them. I was no longer bothered by my mother's cough; I felt only the pain in my hands. I slept a total of two hours a night, from five until seven in the morning. For this I had my aunt Zlata to thank, since she came to spell me every day at dawn. Of course, two hours of sleep was not very much, and it would seem like someone was waking me up as soon as I lay down. But I will never, ever forget my aunt Zlata because of this; I will always think well of her. She is dear to my heart, my pious, smart, and proud aunt.

The months went by, and despite our care, my mother got worse. Her friends told her that she should go to Warsaw to see a professor. "What do the local doctors know?" they said. "Nothing!" But a professor was something else: when a professor examined a patient, he could tell what was going on. My mother let herself be persuaded, and she went off to Warsaw. This was in spring, two weeks before Pesach, so I was left to be a shopkeeper and a housekeeper on my own just before the holiday. But I carried on, hoping that the Warsaw professor would do her some good.

I could hardly wait to get a letter from my mother, which I finally did ten days after she left. She wrote that she had gone to see one Professor Baranovsky, but he had not told her anything; he had simply given her a prescription and told her to come back again in a few days. He had charged ten rubles for the visit, and his assistant another three, and nothing had come of it yet. It had been three days since she had seen him. She had already finished the prescription without seeing any improvement, but perhaps this would come with the next visit. It was very frustrating. God would certainly have compassion for those who prayed, she wrote, but we were sinful people who didn't know the right way to pray. In any case, she wrote, she planned to come home for the last two days of Pesach. The letter ended with these words: "Be well, children; pray to God for your sick mother!" I felt discouraged that the professor had not yet helped her, but I was hopeful for her next appointment.

Meanwhile, I began preparing for Pesach as we did every year when my mother had been well. I whitewashed and cleaned, I put embroidered pillowcases on the cushions and laid the embroidered tablecloth that my grandmother had brought from Rishelevsk on the table, and I even set her porcelain duck sugar bowl on the sideboard. We usually looked forward to Pesach all winter long, and when my mother was well, the whole house seemed cheerful. Now everything felt dark and sad. We held the seder as usual, together with my former tutor Mikhoel the melamed and my tall uncle Izak Meyer, who was living with us. As the youngest child present, my little brother asked my uncle the traditional Four Questions: *Why is this night different from all other nights?* And our hearts were very heavy.

My mother came home for the end of Pesach, together with someone she had met along the way: her younger sister from Rishelevsk, along with her sister's young son. You can't imagine the joy we got from having these guests! Her boy was beautiful and went around dressed like a little prince. My aunt dressed handsomely too, like a noblewoman. They seemed to me like people from a different world. Soon my aunts and cousins and other acquaintances came running and everyone began to kiss each other. The next day, my aunt went out visiting in a black silk dress.

Everyone ran out to gawk at her and at her clothes. A couple of dozen boys ran after her son, and they examined his fine suit with its gold buttons. The diversion with my aunt did not last long, however. She spent a few days with us and then left.

It was again quiet in our home, and I came to realize that my mother was just as sick as before. We began to have those terrible nights again. Then my mother got a letter from her brother in Rishelevsk, in which he wrote that she should travel to the city of Slavuta for the summer. The air was good there, he wrote, and she could drink koumiss, a fermented mare's milk with all kinds of health benefits. He would send her the money to pay for it all. My mother really did not feel like traveling, but she left right away in the hope that it would help. I did not have as much faith in the healing powers of the forests of Slavuta as I had had in the Warsaw professor, but of course I hoped she would see some improvement. The first letters she wrote me were tolerable, but the rest got progressively worse, and the later letters were no longer even written in her hand, but in my uncle's. He wrote that my mother had been in such danger that she had sent for him and my grandmother by telegram. Before we came, he wrote, she thought she was going to die, but now she felt better. As soon as she improved a bit more, my grandmother would bring her home. I received this terrible news Friday night. My little brother and I cried, "Mama!" and everyone came running, but they could hardly calm us down.

The next morning, early on Shabbes, when I went out into the street, I saw small groups of people standing around talking, the women with tears flowing and some blowing their noses. As soon as they saw me, they stopped talking and began to moan. I pretended not to notice, but their pitying voices stung. I could hardly bear those few days until my mother came home, but she returned in the same condition in which she had left, though finally devoid of hope that she would ever regain her health. It seemed that she no longer believed in anything.

A few months went by, and my mother continued to feel unwell. The women began to say that her illness might have come about because of the shock she had received on April Fool's Day the previous year, when Sashke the *panienke* had come to the shul and told my mother our house was on fire. The women advised my mother to call on the *opshprekherin* who lived in Berez, a village that lay four miles from our shtetl. My mother decided to go; she hired a wagon and left for Berez with her old friend Ester-Musha. When they arrived, it turned out that the female *opshprekherin* they had expected was not there, but there was a man—an old gentile of ninety years, who would walk around in the forest for days on end gathering herbs for medicines. He gave my mother some kind of herbal remedy and spoke an incantation over her. He said that her illness was caused by a fright, and to really cure her, someone needed to go and recite an incantation in the very same place where she had been frightened. But since he himself could not travel, he would send one of his friends, a gentile woman. Someone fetched her, and she soon came to terms to go if she was paid two rubles. Of course she was paid what she asked, and they departed with her.

The three of them arrived back home that evening. My mother told me to serve the gentile a good supper and to let her sleep in my bed. I was glad to do so. I gave her all of the meat from our supper and made up a nice bed for her. I had no idea what to do with her, but I hoped that my mother would be healed by her incantations. My grandmother looked askance at the woman, not because she didn't believe in her spells, but because she simply detested a gentile. She could not bring herself to watch while this woman crossed herself in our own home. My grandfather stopped by to inquire after my mother's health, and when he noticed the gentile, he grinned, but so my mother couldn't see. It turns out that he did not believe much in her assistance, but he kept that to himself.

At twelve o'clock midnight, I took the gentile to our shul so she could perform her spells on the threshold and the steps that led up to the women's section. She took along a bit of barley, and she set it on the bottom step and crossed herself over it continuously for perhaps a full hour. I stood there and trembled like a leaf. Does it sound trivial? Standing in our shul at twelve o'clock midnight, just down the road from the Cold Shul, and with a gentile at that, and the gentile crossing herself and crossing the shul! I never divulged this to anyone; I was scared that if people found out, no one would ever want to pray in the shul again. I could hardly wait for her to finish crossing herself so we could go back home. It was a beautiful night; the moon shone so brightly you could gather needles from the ground. Under different circumstances, I would have been happy to stand on the street and look at such a beautiful moon, but that night I was terrified by the gentile, by her crossing herself, and by the Cold Shul.

The next morning, she cooked up a soup from the barley she had crossed and gave it to my mother to eat. I watched my mother eat the soup and thought, if she knew what the gentile had done with that barley, she definitely would not have wanted to eat it.

In the evening, the woman departed, saying that in three days, there would be an improvement in my mother's illness. Each day dragged on for us like a year. We could hardly wait for the fourth day, but when it arrived, there was still no improvement. My mother was already saying that all avenues of assistance had been exhausted and that nothing would help. She had heard about intercessors appearing in a dream, she said; a grandmother, a grandfather or an aunt would visit from the world to come and bring something or say something to help, but none had come for her. My grandmother broke in and told a story she had heard in Rabinsk. A woman there became sick, and she went to see all the doctors, and none of them helped.

She too lost all hope of ever being well again. But one of her grandmothers came to her in a dream, and her grandmother brought her a bit of herb wrapped in a packet of paper and said, "Here, my daughter, drink up this medicine, and you'll be well." In the morning, the sick woman remembered her dream, and when she lifted her pillow, she found a little packet of herbs. She drank the herbal remedy and soon regained her health.

My grandmother's story made a strong impression on me. If only God would send us such a miracle, I thought—and perhaps he will! Who knew? Every morning, I looked under my mother's pillow. But my efforts were in vain; I never found a thing. I grew angry with my great-grandmother and my aunts in the world to come, because they had forgotten about my mother, and I stopped looking under her pillow.

The summer passed and the night of the first penitential *selichos* prayer service arrived. At dawn, when Moyshke the shammes was waking everyone for the second service, my mother was still up and coughing; she had not yet been to sleep. My grandmother was off at *selichos* in shul, and I figured it wouldn't hurt to say *selichos* myself and have a good cry. I sat down to pray, and tears started flowing from my eyes as from a wellspring. My heart was easier afterward. I felt as if I had talked my problems over with God, and that he had heard me out. Surely he would give me a better year than the last.

My grandmother was immersed in piety from the first day of the month of Elul; she prayed all the time, read *tkhines*, and fasted every day. On Rosh Hashanah, someone brought the shofar to our home so my mother could hear it. Erev Yom Kippur arrived, and my grandmother didn't know what to do first. There were perhaps ten kinds of prayers to be said, with another *tkhine* every hour, and also the *kapores* ceremony of atonement. And then there was the candle making. This was a boisterous ritual where the women got together to make large wax candles, which were used to create a connection with their ancestors so they would invoke God's mercy for us. Some ten or fifteen women gathered at our neighbor Malke-Rokhl's, and everyone brought the small pieces of wax or bits of braided havdalah candles that were left over from the entire year, and each woman made a huge candle. The candle making was such a tumult that you could go deaf from the racket. Some of the women shaped their wax in a kneading trough, while others set their candles to dry on a stand while they wailed *tkhines*. Malke-Rokhl outshouted them all. She had to talk to everyone: she asked this one how much the wax had cost her; the second, if her tzimmes had turned out well for dinner; the third, if she had a choice *kapores*; and other such things. By the time each candle was finished, everyone had wished each other all sorts of good things, however trivial; sometimes I thought only a mad dog would have cared about the ridiculous things they said. But this did no harm to the work at hand. The *tkhines* were wailed, and they laid wicks in the candles to honor the souls of our holy ancestors. My grandmother laid a wick for her own mother and prayed for God to quickly restore us to happier times.

My grandmother finished making her candle, which she stuck in a large pot filled with sand. Then my brother and I got dressed in our holiday clothes to go visit our grandfather, so he could bless us for the new year. We met my uncle there, a tall young man, my grandfather's only remaining son, who had brought all his children for my grandfather to bless too.

I still remember my grandfather's blessing that year. I can't express how happy I felt, looking at him. He was robed in a white kittel, and his beard and bushy eyebrows were just as white as his robe. But his eyes gleamed with a dark luster and radiated limitless faith, truth, and goodness. He saw so far; he perceived everyone in the house, and under his gaze, one felt protected from all malice. My grandfather loved everyone and had no enemies. In a word, he was justice personified. When he blessed us that Erev Yom Kippur, he laid both of his hands on our heads and murmured a prayer. His eyes shone like a mirror, and his figure, which was a bit stooped with age, straightened, his head held high and proud. In that moment, he looked like an angel. It was an unusually beautiful day. The sun was already quite low, and some rays shone through the window and fell upon my grandfather while he stood and blessed us. A sunbeam lingered on his face and was reflected in his gleaming eyes. I was mesmerized, and I saw in his eyes a sea of light, as if the sun itself had settled in them, or as if a candle were burning right in his head. I trembled with awe.

My grandfather asked me how my mother was doing. When I told him that my mother had had a bad night, he thought for a minute and said, "Come, children, I will go and bless your mother, so she should regain her health and finish raising her children!" My grandfather came to our house and blessed my mother. He laid his hands on her head while he prayed, but his eyes were no longer lit up; his figure was again bent, and his head drooped. Two big tears rolled down over his white beard. What had become of his earlier pride and tranquility? It turned out that he felt that he was blessing her for the last time, and that she would not live to see another Yom Kippur. My mother also cried a good bit and thanked my grandfather for his blessing. My grandfather said a few more prayers over her before leaving for shul, where everyone was waiting for him.

Early the next morning, I went to shul to consult my grandfather about what my mother should eat on Yom Kippur. My grandfather gave me strict orders to call in a gentile woman to cook a fresh soup, since someone as ill as my mother should not fast. I went home and reported this to my mother. At my words, she gave a start and she said, "What do you mean, a fresh soup on Yom Kippur? God protect us from such a sin!"

"But you mustn't fast," I said.

My mother answered that she would do what the rabbi in Seltz had told her to do the previous year: instead of a fresh-cooked meal, she would eat a small piece of honey cake, the size of half an egg, every half hour. All the women who came to check on her approved of the Seltzer rabbi's decree.

We got through Yom Kippur and Sukkos and made it to the joyous holiday of Simchas Torah that fall. Everyone in the shtetl was cheerful, but it was sad in our home. My mother said that in a year's time, she wouldn't mind being so poor that she didn't have the smallest piece of bread, if only she could be healthy. I said that I wouldn't mind if I never had a pillow again; if my mother could be healthy, I would sleep very comfortably all night long, even on the bare ground.

8

Yosef

My mother's health got even worse after Sukkos. She started up again with the doctors and left for Seltz with my grandmother for a couple of months. This time I was not left on my own, but with a servant named Sheyne Gitl. Sheyne Gitl was a local woman, born and bred in the shtetl, whose husband had died young. When her husband had died, her father-in-law, Khayim the smith, took in her children, but Sheyne Gitl was left to go live among strangers.

Living with me was not what you would call living among strangers, however—it was as if she were living in her own home. I was such a good mistress that I didn't even know how to treat her, and I never dared to tell her what to do. It was just the opposite: she bossed me around. But whatever she did was fine with me, because I loved her. She was a quiet and pious person, and I believed she was as honest as God himself. My aunt Zlata, who was more pragmatic and smarter than I, understood that it was to Sheyne Gitl's advantage to have a naive boss like me. My aunt began keeping an eye on her, and indeed, she soon noticed what she suspected, that Sheyne Gitl was helping herself to things here and there. My aunt was no fool, but it wasn't her style to confront her directly; instead, she spread the word discreetly about the thefts. It wasn't long before the rumors got back to Sheyne Gitl.

Sheyne Gitl strongly denied the accusation. She had been disgraced in front of her family, so she raised a ruckus and had a falling out with my aunt Zlata. I couldn't bear it. I was upset that my aunt had insulted her. Was Sheyne Gitl really stealing from me? I didn't want to believe it; I simply couldn't imagine that piety and honesty were two completely different things. I felt guilty and was ashamed to look Sheyne Gitl in the eye, and I worried that God would punish my aunt Zlata for unjustifiably insulting such a virtuous soul. I sought some way to make it up to her and constantly made excuses for her, but when I defended her, she cursed my aunt right to my face. I felt even worse then, and I began to look for other means to appease her. Soon I found one: I sat up all night and sewed several little shirts for her sons. Sheyne Gitl was very pleased, and I felt happy that I had paid off my debt. And I was sure, having done so, that God would not punish my aunt Zlata for her great sin. Sheyne Gitl was not satisfied, however, and as it turns out, she did indeed help herself from my purse. Nonetheless, when all was said and done, she was a nice young woman. She was a good cook and worked all day for me and my brother as well as for her own young children.

Since Sheyne Gitl was taking care of our home and doing all the cooking, I lived like a princess; I was only a shopkeeper. I finally had enough free time to read from time to time. The problem was, there was nothing to read. I had already read all the books in the shtetl three times, and I knew them all by heart. I began to contemplate how to get some new material. I finally decided on a difficult strategy, though at first I was frightened by the idea: I decided to approach Khatzkel the coachman and ask him to bring me a book from Seltz.

I waited a long time for Khatzkel to be in a good mood, which was rare now that he had married Khaye-Beyla and become rich. He had very little patience for me. He had to put up with the big shopkeepers and proprietors, and when he was home, he vented all his anger and bitterness on me as a little shopkeeper. I always kept silent as a kitten and listened to his stream of invective, but whenever he threw a glance at me, I trembled with fear.

Compared to other people, I had a lot of self-confidence, but there was one other person who made me just as nervous as Khatzkel: the excise tax collector. In those days, there were excise taxes on things like sugar, tobacco, and matches, and I had more of these illicit things in the store than legal ones, since if you wanted to run a store in a small shtetl by the book, as the tax collector would have it, you would have to pay more for the license than you could earn in an entire year. This is why I was so scared, and why I felt so guilty when he was around. I never actually saw him, because as soon as I heard the tinkling of his little bell, I would turn pale, grab all the illicit merchandise and my little book of psalms, and hide in the cellar, entrusting the store to our boarder, Basia-Reyzl, who whispered a specific *tkhine* by heart when the tax collector came through, her teeth chattering in fright.

Meanwhile, I would stay in the cellar, trembling and reciting psalms and praying to God that the tax collector would get drunk at the priest's and not have the strength to go around to the shops. My book of psalms always helped. The tax collector would indeed drink at the priest's for a few hours and then depart. Only after I heard the little bell as he drove off would I creep out from the cellar with all the illicit merchandise and my little book. Only when I felt that he was far away would I finally breathe freely and laugh at myself for having been so frightened. When I went back in the store, I always found my grandfather sitting there, because as soon as he had heard the little bell, he would come rushing over to calm me down and take care of everything.

Why should the tax collector cause so much anxiety over something so silly, I used to think; would the tsar really be so poor if the shopkeepers in the little shtetls didn't pay the license fee for all their merchandise? What should the poor shopkeepers do if their stores couldn't bear the expense? And how many mitzvahs the tax collector could earn, if only he were a good person! Everyone would bless him and pray to God on his behalf. He was given "presents," to be sure, but this was the wrong kind of giving, with such motivation! I used to think that if I had been in his place, I would have gone to all the shopkeepers and said: "Sell what you want, little Jews, I won't say a word!" This would have made him a good person, instead of coming with his little bell and frightening the entire shtetl.

There was good reason to be afraid of the tax inspector, but why should I be anxious about Khatzkel the coachman? After all, when he brought you something, you paid him good money for it. But he had a short temper, and he was always blowing up at someone. Nonetheless, whenever he had to make a run to Seltz, a group of shopkeepers would gather around him, each trying to figure out how best to ask him to bring what they needed.

Why was everyone so eager to do business with Khatzkel, when there were other coachmen who were just as eager to earn a commission? Eydl was right when she said that everyone had changed how they treated Khatzkel after he had married into Khaye-Beyla's fortune; no one had been so eager to turn to him when he had been poor. Khaye-Beyla stood next to him now, observing the crowd with disdain and putting on ever more airs, looking at the group of

foolish people with a satisfied smirk. The shopkeepers tolerated everything from streams of invective to
curses just to prostrate themselves before him. The
other coachmen weren't bad people, or nearly as hos-
tile as he was; in fact, they were grateful to anyone
who gave them business. Nonetheless, nobody went
to them.

It was clear in my case that I had to turn to
Khatzkel, and for something as annoying as fetch-
ing me a book. When it was my turn to approach
him, I felt my heart pounding like a hammer; I would
be lucky if I wasn't met with his angry look and his
acerbic words. I gathered my courage and asked if
he could bring me a book from the library in Seltz.
If he had to pay a deposit, I told him, he should pay
it, and I would pay him back and pay for his efforts
as well. I was lucky. At first, he equivocated and said
that he didn't have time to devote to such foolishness, but then God softened his heart for a minute,
and he promised to stop by the library. I thanked him
sincerely, quivering with joy, but it seemed to be too
little. I can't begin to express what I felt for Khatzkel
just then. In an instant, I forgot all the insults that I
had always put up with, and I promptly became his
best friend. He turned dearer to me than if he had
been my own brother. If I hadn't been so scared of
Khaye-Beyla, I would have given him a kiss.

During the time when Khatzkel was on the road,
I prayed for him to come home safe and sound and
not have any kind of accident en route, and I counted

the minutes he was away. When I saw that he had returned, I rejoiced as if he were my father from the world to come. I didn't try to get the book right away, however. As soon as Khatzkel got home, no one was allowed even to speak to him, or he would get angry. You had to wait until he had eaten and slept before you could hope to approach him. I waited even longer, because I didn't mind deferring to him, and because I was still embarrassed to have asked him for the book. I was also scared that Khaye-Beyla would speak ill of me to others and say that I had an empty head: my mother was lying sick in Seltz, and all I could think about was books. And so I kept silent and waited for Khatzkel. Finally I saw something intriguing in his window, wrapped in paper. I went and asked Khatzkel if I could see what it was. He confirmed that it was indeed my book, and said he'd gone to a lot of trouble to get it, because I had written that they should send me only Shomer's novel, *The Convict*, and he had to pay a ruble deposit for it. I didn't even hear his last words. I tore off the paper to find a fat novel of four hundred pages—so much to read! How wonderful! The bold words on the first page, *The Convict*, flashed at me. I grabbed the book and ran out without even saying goodbye.

But as I dashed out, I noticed Khaye-Beyla looking after me askance. I understood from her expression that she had something to say, so when I left her house, I stopped to listen. As soon as I closed the door, I heard her speaking to my old teacher, Berl the melamed. "What do you think about that girl?" she said. "She must really be thinking about her sick mother a lot, if she can do so well without her. She must want her mother to die even sooner so she'll be free to read books and other such things. What's going to become of her, if at fourteen she's already burning down the world?" Berl waited until she was finished and then answered her so well that I danced for joy on the other side of the door. He told her that I was the way I was because I had such a good head, because I was intelligent and understood so much. "If she had been a boy, she would have grown up to be a scholar, just like her father," he said. Khaye-Beyla grew quiet, listening to Berl's opinion of me. She was smart enough to realize that the melamed knew a lot more than she did, so she agreed that I was clever, but she said that I was always daydreaming, and I didn't even know what planet I was on.

As I walked home, I wondered how Khaye-Beyla would be able to look me in the eye the next day, having said this about me today. But I soon forgot all about her, because I had the book. I finished doing all my chores and sat down to read. It was quiet in the house. My little brother was already asleep, and Sheyne Gitl sat and dozed next to the spinning wheel. The spindle had fallen from her hand, and she had fallen into a sweet sleep, as you could hear throughout the whole room. Otherwise it was completely silent. I was pleased that no one was bothering me and

I could read in peace, and I completely forgot that I was supposed to get up early the next morning.

The clock had already struck two and I was still reading. I happened to glance out the window and began to shudder. The entire shtetl was dark and silent as a graveyard. I heard the clock ticking and Sheyne Gitl snoring. I was startled by my own reflection, which I had caught sight of in the window, and I began to feel afraid. I called out to Sheyne Gitl. She was frightened when I roused her, and she rushed over and asked what was wrong. I answered that I had seen a person standing outside the window. She looked at my pale, frightened face, then at the clock, which had just struck two-thirty, and finally at my open book. It was clear she understood the situation. She spat at me several times, *tu tu tu*, and began to chastise me for having such an empty head: "All you think about is this foolishness," she scolded. "Look around you! You don't have a father, your mother is sick, and you're not a child anymore; you should understand your situation, and all you can think about is reading books and sitting up all night. In the morning, you won't be able to lift your head. Shame on you! You think you're so smart. It's not for nothing that people say that all your talent is wasted; knowledge and wisdom in an empty keg. Go; go to bed. You can part with your precious book!"

I obeyed her right away and hid the book under my pillow so that she wouldn't see; I was anxious that she might burn it. I went to bed, and for the first time in my life, I forgot to say the *Shema* before I went to sleep.

The next morning, I remembered right away that I had forgotten to say the *Shema*. I was so upset that I felt a pang in my heart. Khaye-Beyla was right to say that I was a daydreamer. Was it really true that books could lead one astray? No, I didn't believe it. What did one thing have to do with the other? One could be devout and read books too. The fact that I'd forgotten to say the *Shema* last night was just that and nothing more. Sometimes you just forget. I was certain that it wouldn't happen again.

I went around the entire day in a daze. The characters from *The Convict* stood before me and followed me wherever I went. They were as dear and precious to me as if they were family, as if I had known them for years. I couldn't wait to get back to the book, because the story's climax was still coming up, but I had to wait for that happy moment. Today was Thursday, and I had a lot of work to do. The shop was so busy I didn't know whom to take care of first, and in the evening, when it was quiet, I had to deny myself the pleasure of sitting down with the book. What Jewish woman could let herself do so, on a Thursday evening? To say nothing about Friday, because who had time for anything on a Friday? But in return, there was Friday evening—such a nice, long evening! Even in summer, when sunset was so late, there was plenty of time to stay up after the start of Shabbes, because

I didn't have to get up early the next morning. And the pleasure of the next day was just indescribable. I could also read on Saturday evening. But oh, how I hated Sunday, with all of its drunk gentiles!

I made it to Shabbes, thank God. After blessing the candles, I went to take my book from the cupboard. Suddenly I remembered about the *Kabbalas Shabbes*, the Friday evening prayers to greet the Shabbes, and I frowned. I glared at my women's prayer book; I really didn't feel like praying. But I summoned my strength, opened my prayer book, and began chanting the *Lekha Dodi* using the same sweet tune my mother always used. I loved the Hebrew in the *Kabbalas Shabbes*, with its beautiful melody. Something about every word felt like sweet music to me. Every word called forth another hymn, and the words and the singing fused together; sweet melodies rang in my ears and flowed through my entire body. I felt somehow closer to God, more elevated, more beautiful, and happier than at any other time; I felt as if I were floating high above as I said these prayers. But that Friday evening I did not fly very high. I did enjoy the singing, as usual, but I noticed myself saying the prayers a bit faster than usual, because the entire time I felt my attention drawn to the cupboard, which was locked for the first time in its life.

In locking the cupboard, I had offended the pious Sheyne Gitl, though I wasn't aware of it at the time. I trusted her as if she were my own sister; that is, I trusted her with everything except the book, but I wouldn't have trusted my own sister with that either. I guarded the key to the cupboard and kept it always in my pocket. Whenever Sheyne Gitl needed something from the cupboard, she yelled at me for locking it. What had she stolen from me? she asked. I turned red and didn't know how to answer. But I still didn't give her the key.

I could hardly wait for supper to be over so I could begin reading. My little brother also sat down with a book, since he loved to read too. He always laughed at my books: a girl reading, just like a man! As if she has any idea what she's reading! His slights really offended me, and we often came to blows about this. Now, when he saw that I was reading one of Shomer's novels, he grinned, but he kept silent. I knew that Shomer's novels were considered trash in some circles, but I was not interested in my brother's opinion. I was interested only in one thing: what would happen to the characters next? I sat up very late that Friday evening; I might have stayed up all night, but luckily the lamp ran out of kerosene.

I undressed and closed my eyes, spooked by the shadows the candles were casting on the wall. I said the *Shema* while lying in bed. My mouth said the words, because I knew them so well, but I was preoccupied; through my closed eyes, I saw Shomer's characters as if they were real. I was completely caught up in their lives. I sensed their joys and sorrows; I felt sorry for the ones who were suffering and envious of the ones who were happy. But I had not yet reached the end of the book, and I trembled to think it might end badly.

Later, when I did finish the book, I was delighted that everything ended so well. Oh, how I beamed with joy at its wonderful end! The just people who had been unlucky ended up happy, and the hypocritical criminals were punished, each according to their merit, and all was right with the world.

Shomer's book revolutionized my thinking. I learned things from it I had never even imagined earlier. I learned that a boy who sat day and night over the Talmud in a study hall could afterward study to qualify as a doctor. I couldn't begin to imagine how a simple yeshiva boy could become a doctor, but if Shomer had written it, it must be true; he must have seen it with his own eyes. In a casual note, I thought to myself, someone could jot down a lie now and then, but in a book, this just couldn't be—this must be truth itself.

But there was one thing I simply couldn't fathom: could there really be rich Jewish barons, as depicted in the book? Did these people exist? They must be really exceptional. I wondered what their lives were like. They ate and drank so well and wore silk clothes and slept until noon all the time. And their children! Each one had a maid, a nanny, or a governess, and they could speak a variety of languages. People like doctors, lawyers, and university students were quite ordinary guests in their home. The children got presents every day, and not just tchotchkes either, and they were cherished and treated with respect. Nobody got angry with them; even when they misbehaved, no one punished or reprimanded them. Instead, their mother gave them a kiss to calm them down. What lucky children!

The Jewish baron in Shomer's novel had two children. What if God had made me the baron's daughter? I would be better than the others, I decided. I would not run away from the poor the way they did. Moreover, I would be a lot more pious. Even in the midst of such opulence, I thought, it would be nice to be religious. I imagined what a fine Shabbes they could have, if only they observed it, and what nice Pesach, Shavuos, and Sukkos celebrations. But they didn't observe any of these traditions. I pictured a sukkah in a gorgeous garden, but what did they need a sukkah for, when they had such beautiful gazebos in their garden already? And what did they need Shavuos for, since they ate butter cookies with their tea all summer? Pesach was also nothing special for them, since they drank wine all year, and plenty of it. What good were the holidays, if every day was already a celebration?

I did want to know if they ever thought about death, amidst all their heretical whims. When they died, their little part of this sweet world would vanish like a dream, and how would they answer to the celestial council of justice? There, they would pay for it all, I thought, and get the vengeance they deserved; I remembered the stories from the *Shevet Musar* about how wicked people were punished in hell. But this did not assuage me; I could not stop envying them for their good lives here on earth. I made up my mind that it would be better to stop thinking about them altogether.

There was one character in Shomer's novel I could not forget, however; he followed me like a shadow wherever I went. This was Dovidl, the protagonist of the story. Dovidl is a poor yeshiva boy, a great scholar, both pious and handsome, with smoldering eyes. He has a very keen mind and is ordained as a rabbi at eighteen. The head of the yeshiva, Reb Zemach, has a very high opinion of him. Dovidl sits day and night over the Talmud; he never steps out into the world. Unexpectedly, through an extraordinary coincidence, he ends up at the Jewish baron's house. He falls in love with the baron's daughter, the beautiful, educated, and rich Marietta, and she falls in love with him too. He is frightened by his love for Marietta and wants to run away from her and her beauty and wealth, because at every turn, he has a feeling that she's laughing at him, with his old-fashioned kaftan and his *peyes*, his long sidelocks. He wonders how she can possibly pay attention to him, especially when she in turn is loved by a rich university student named Zunnenflam. How insignificant he is compared to Zunnenflam! And how he hates Zunnenflam for ridiculing him in front of Marietta. But Marietta pays no attention to Zunnenflam. She becomes attached to Dovidl when she sees him intuitively understand some beautiful music. She gives him some money, and he steals away from the yeshiva and from Reb Zemach, who had betrothed him to his own annoying daughter a couple of years earlier. Dovidl goes off to study at a university in a big city too, wearing a student's uniform complete with an overcoat with golden buttons. When he returns to the baron's place during his summer break, he seems like a nobleman, with language to match, and he speaks eloquently about his deep love for Marietta. His triumph over Zunnenflam is complete. He marries Marietta and ends up becoming a rich doctor.

I was very jealous of Marietta for having such a fiancé, but at first I thought she was crazy. I could not imagine how she could renounce the handsome, rich Zunnenflam and fall in love with a poor, simple yeshiva boy. However, it turned out later that even though Zunnenflam was an aristocrat, he was depraved; by contrast, even after raising himself up, Dovidl retained his good character. Marietta really was a smart young lady, in that she understood early on that such a simple boy could grow up to be a handsome, noble university student.

Nonetheless, I would have wanted a fiancé like Zunnenflam. It didn't bother me that his character was corrupt. No one would see how he behaved at home, but by contrast, out in public—what respectability there would be in having such a handsome, rich, educated husband! Moreover, when he walked around in his university uniform, he was truly a joy to behold. That uniform made a big impression on me. I would not have liked Zunnenflam if he hadn't been wearing it; he would have seemed too ordinary and not like a student at all.

Now, wherever I went, it was Zunnenflam who followed me with his golden buttons. I was afraid to even think about Dovidl, because he was Marietta's fiancé, and I felt that it would hurt her. My heart went out to her; she had already been through enough before she won him, and I didn't want to take him away from her. But Zunnenflam was free as a bird; I could think about him as much as I wanted.

What would happen if a university student were to suddenly fall in love with me? I would go crazy with pleasure, and the whole shtetl would just burst, looking at his handsome uniform. All the girls would be jealous. In truth, my mother and my grandfather would not want me to marry someone who was not a practicing Jew, but I could manage. Why shouldn't it happen? In one of Shomer's books, a prince had fallen in love with a forest-child, and in another, the son of a Jewish baron, Yosef, had fallen in love with a simple seamstress. And I was not just some nobody— you should excuse the comparison, but I was far from being a seamstress whose mother was a cook! The student would have the right to ask us, or rather, to ask my grandfather and my mother, who would certainly feel that such a match was beneath me. But the footing did not seem so unequal to me, and when I thought about it, I trembled all over with joy.

I began to wonder how I could meet a university student, when no one from our shtetl had ever laid eyes on one. I would have to think about this. It occurred to me that I might find a student in Seltz—a big city like that must have the goods. There was no university in Seltz, but there were enough wealthy men there who sent their children far away to study at universities in Moscow, Saint Petersburg, or Kiev—and in the summers, of course, the students would come home. Because I went to Seltz so frequently, perhaps I would meet one on the street.

But my work was fruitless. I never saw a real live student in Seltz, no matter how hard I looked. Whenever I saw a young man in a uniform, I wondered if he might be a student, but I didn't let myself be fooled. I always asked a relative or friend who he was, and I was always told that it was only a bureaucrat. Then one time, when I was walking on the street with one of my cousins who studied at the yeshiva in Seltz, we met a tall, blond young man, who walked with a bold stride. My cousin pointed him out and said that he was the son of a local magnate, a university student who studied somewhere far away. I fairly began to tremble. I stared at the young man and asked in astonishment: why doesn't he have golden buttons on his jacket? My cousin answered that when he was home, he didn't like to wear his student uniform; he preferred a simple suit. I had never imagined that a person could renounce such handsome clothes. The fellow pleased me all the same, though of course I had expected to see something even finer. If he had been wearing a uniform, I thought, he would have been a thousand times more handsome. No, for me, this wasn't a real student; I wanted to see someone in a uniform with golden buttons. Nonetheless, I didn't lose hope. God would surely send me a student, perhaps in some completely unexpected way.

In the meantime, I read a lot of thick books, full of romance. I read lots of novels by Shomer and a few other writers, but I don't remember most of the others; aside from Shomer, they didn't really interest me. Some of the books that made a strong impression on me were *The Blind Orphan Girl* and *The World Reversed* by Shomer, and *A Stone on the Road* by Yankev Dinezon. I also remember *The Dark Young Man* by Dinezon very well, because I retold it several times for the girls in my shtetl. Their eyes flowed with tears, hearing me tell it, and I was elated. In the moment, I even forgot that it was Dinezon who had set the words down; it felt like I had written it myself.

Reading all these long novels made me crazy. I just wanted to fall in love with someone, and not just anyone—only a student would do, or a doctor would have been fine too. Whenever I had a bit of free time, I'd stand in front of our broken mirror and study myself, to see how tall I was, and to see if I looked old enough to be courted, as we used to say. I began to cinch my clothes around the waist. I gave myself a haircut with bangs, which I thought suited me, and I started to dress in clothes to complement my face.

I liked light colors best. When no one was there, I stood in front of the mirror for hours and practiced making a sweet little smile, exactly as a certain character had greeted her beloved.

The more I read, the more confused I got. I completely forgot where I was and lived only in my imagination. I constantly fantasized that some rich student would suddenly come and fall in love with me and whisk me far away to a big city. We would get married there, and my husband would take me to fancy palaces with pretty furniture and mirrors. I would go for drives in a carriage with modern rubber tires. I would go to the theater every night and then sleep until noon. My servants would help me present a grand appearance. I had to have a lackey and a doorman; I wouldn't have it any other way. And if I felt like it, I would simply go off to Italy for a few months. It was a real paradise there! I swooned to read descriptions of its pretty meadows, forests, and rivers. Here at home, I figured I would buy my mother a summer house in Volhynia, somewhere in a pine forest. I would send my little brother off to study in a big city, and I would settle in to be a doctor's wife. My husband's reception would be full of patients who would sit and wait until he could see them, and I would pass through proudly all the time, so everyone could see how happy I was. I would ask him to care for the poor for free. I myself would be strictly religious. I would prepare the Shabbes and holiday celebrations in a pretty parlor, and I would place copies of the Talmud in beautiful bindings in my husband's large library. Friday evenings I would say the blessing over the candles in large silver candlesticks, and I would see to it that my husband would observe Shabbes; he would say kiddush over a large silver cup. Well, he might have to travel to see a sick patient on Shabbes, but was that sacrilegious? I would also raise my children in piety. What more could I do, other than give to charity?

There was one thing that troubled me, however: if I didn't wear a *sheytl* after I married, then in the world to come, I would have to hang by my hair for years on end. That would really not be good. But if I did wear one, that would also not be good—there was something unseemly about a doctor's wife in a wig. I wanted to appear respectable among my modern acquaintances, the intelligentsia, and a nice doctor's wife I'd make, in a *sheytl*! I would have to get advice from my Herr Doctor. Whatever he told me to do would be correct. If he said that I didn't have to wear a wig, I would lay the sin on him. It would be just one among others, I was sure, and I thought this was a very good plan indeed.

And so I plotted out my world of respectability and wealth for generations upon generations, because how could a doctor's children grow up to be simple or poor? It was all well and good, but there was still no student to be found. Instead, I remained in my fantasy world and constantly invented new details about my pious, refined future.

I *still* could not find a student. But in the end, God did not forsake me: "my student" came to me on a bright, beautiful day. Who was this fellow? He was one of my near relations from my father's side, who lived in Seltz.

My grandfather had a lot of nieces and nephews in Seltz, all of whom were quite rich. He went to see them frequently, and they always welcomed him warmly. Whenever he came home, however, he couldn't stop complaining that they weren't raising their children to be Jewish, and that they themselves were already not as religious as their fathers, the *tsaddikim*. Among these relatives, it turns out there was a student studying in Moscow to be a doctor, who came home to his parents every summer. My grandfather had just seen him, and he liked him very much. I listened while my grandfather told my grandmother how smart and educated he was. Even though he wasn't religious, my grandfather said, he did love Jews. He loved the land of Israel and was even thinking about going there.

Now this was a nice scenario, I thought—a student in the land of Israel; this had just the right presentability for a doctor's wife in a wig. Of course there was a concern that he might be a bit meshuga, but nonetheless, he was a student. Why wouldn't we make a good match? Our pedigree was of course the same; my father had been an even greater scholar than his. Furthermore, I was educated too; I had read quite a lot and not just anything: I had even read all of Shomer's works. I hadn't yet learned any Russian, but I could still do so; it wasn't exactly like studying Talmud. Next, I was a bit too young, but that didn't matter. I was already fourteen years old, but I looked twenty, and if I wore dark clothes with a belt, I looked all grown up. Moreover, by the time he finished studying at the university, I would be eighteen. Perfect. As it says in the Torah, one should marry at eighteen. Finally, regarding looks—I didn't worry. I was no beauty, but I wasn't ugly either. He would definitely like me.

And so I finally had someone specific to fantasize about. Even though I never laid eyes on him, I thought about him all the time. I imagined I was already in love with him, and it went without saying that he loved me too. But I couldn't tell anyone about it, that was certain.

I felt real love from my student. I imagined him as if he were that blond young man that I had seen in the street in Seltz, but in a uniform, of course. He became my paragon. I couldn't sleep; I thought about him all night long, and when I did fall asleep, he appeared in my dreams. I got through my days with the memory of those wonderful, sweet dreams. I remember one in particular, where I walked arm in arm with my student, whom I called "my dear Yosef," the name of one of Shomer's protagonists. We walked together throughout the shtetl, and everyone was jealous of me for having such a fiancé. I walked so proudly in my dream that in real life, I fell out of bed and really banged myself up. But what are a few bruises after a dream like that? My mind had to have something to ruminate on, or I would go crazy. I didn't need much; a bit of a dream was enough to work with. I came up with the rest myself, and I created an entire world with all kinds of people and events.

Soon after that wonderful dream, I received a terrible letter from my mother. She had become even weaker, she said, and her letter was filled with thoughts about death. I sobbed all day long, feeling bitter and forlorn. I wanted to tell someone my troubles, but who could I talk to? If my "friends" were already saying I wanted to be rid of my mother, then how would it look to them? It would be better if I kept my troubles locked away in my heart and made do with crying myself out.

That evening, when my little brother was reading some kind of book in Hebrew, I sat down to a long, four-part Yiddish novel. I wanted to chase away my troubles by reading, but I couldn't concentrate. My mother's letter, so rife with death, would not let me relax. My brother and I read it over again, and we both had another good cry. We didn't speak a single word. We were both suffering, and we understood each other without talking. He quit reading and soon went to bed, and I stayed up by myself. I felt such pain, such anguish, that a cold shiver ran through my bones. Who could I pour my heart out to? Who could comfort me? And then I remembered my dear Yosef, my romantic paragon. I felt a kind of lightness, a warmth in my heart. How he would console me! He would truly understand my pain!

I seized a sheet of paper and wrote him a letter, pouring out my anguished heart. I told him how badly I was doing, and how much I loved him. When I finished, I was shocked. The words "Dear Yosef" stood before my eyes, and the letter was well written. Then it occurred to me that I wanted an answer from him. I picked up another sheet of paper and wrote myself an answer full of consolation and love. I was amazed it came out so well. I wondered what Malke would say if she read it. Why not show it to her? I would try to trick her and see if she would figure it out. With this in mind, I went to bed.

The next day, I invited Malke to spend the night with me, because I had something to tell her, a big secret. Malke could hardly wait for everyone to go to sleep. At last we were alone, and I made her swear by all that is holy that she would not tell a soul. She swore by God himself, and I showed her Yosef's answer to me. She read the letter, her mouth hanging open and her eyes wide. I saw that she wanted to ask something, but she couldn't; her head was spinning. I told her that when I had been with my grandfather in Seltz, he had introduced me to this student, who was one of his nephews. He was very handsome. He was studying in Moscow to be a doctor and would finish in a few years, and then he would marry me. When she heard these words, she looked as if she was going to pass out. Finally she came to and began pelting me with questions: When did he start writing me letters? Had he sent me any presents? After the wedding, would I really live in Seltz? That was the worst for her. She was consumed with jealousy that I would be a doctor's wife and live nearby in Seltz, where everyone great and small in our shtetl would see how happy I was. She, Malke, would arrive with Khatzkel the coachman in his narrow wagon with all his sacks and bundles, and I would pull up opposite in an expensive phaeton with my doctor at my side, all stylish and dolled up. I would frown and not even look at Khatzkel's wagon, not understanding how I too could have once ridden in that same little cart.

We talked all night. We agreed that she should come spend the following night too, and I would show her the answer I would write to him. She went off with her head hanging low. It turned out that, when she got home, she immediately told her mother, Eydl. Eydl was as astonished as she was and just as jealous, but whereas Malke had been stunned into silence when she first heard, her mother spoke right up, saying, "Of all the luck! What a godsend to be handed down from on high! A child of fourteen? She's a complete zero, nothing but a crazy chatterbox, and to have such an opportunity! *She's* going to be a doctor's wife?!"

In the middle of this rant, Mera the seamstress showed up at Eydl's. Mera was a tall, skinny girl, who had lived in Rabinsk for some years while learning how to sew, and who always talked about the marvels of the big city. She knew a lot of love stories about milliners and pharmacists and doctors and lawyers; her stories were similar to Shomer's novels. She was completely taken with big-city life. She often served as a cheerful audience for Eydl. Through Malke, I'd become friends with her too, though my aunt Zlata felt strongly that it was beneath my dignity to befriend a granddaughter of Mendl Ber the furrier. But what could you do with a disagreeable child like me? In any case, Mera showed up just at the right time, because who knew more about love in the big city? Eydl and Malke immediately told her about my romance.

Mera listened to the whole story and explained that it could certainly happen, and what was the big to-do? The pedigree was of course the same, and he liked her. And about the lack of money for a dowry? Come on, that was no problem. Of course a man like that could have gotten ten thousand rubles for a dowry. But he was probably thinking, what's ten thousand rubles for a man like him? God would send him some rich businessmen as patients, and then he'd have his ten thousand rubles. The whole thing was completely reasonable. "You'll see," Mera said, "how a small-shtetl girl will become an aristocratic lady. She'll learn right away. I've seen such things many times, so I'm not a bit surprised."

As Mera told me later, Eydl and Malke hung their heads when they heard these words; they were forced to accept what she said. But Eydl simply couldn't remain silent, and she shot a question up to God: "Isn't

Malke prettier than she is? Malke would be better suited to have a doctor fall in love with her. What did someone like him see in *her*?"

Mera took my side, but she couldn't keep the secret to herself. She told her sister right away, who also agreed that it was an appropriate match, since she too had spent some years in a big city. A few days later, there were several other girls who knew about it too. They all gossiped about my lucky match and said I was fortunate indeed to be engaged at fourteen.

I wrote my fiancé twice a month, sometimes more. Malke was surprised how much he loved me, because he answered me the minute he got my letters. One time, she asked me to write him a bit about her and to tell him that she loved me very much, and to send him her regards. I obeyed her, and soon after, she received a very nice thank you for her greeting. He also asked her to console me when I had a bad spell, and he told her she should visit me often. She shouldn't let me be distressed, because that was bad for one's health. He promised to reciprocate in good time. Malke was very pleased. She obeyed him and devoted herself to looking after me.

Meanwhile, it popped into my head to tell Malke that my Yosef had a kind of telescope that he could see me with, whenever he wanted. "That's nothing new; all doctors have such telescopes," said Mera's sister. Malke didn't doubt for an instant that this might not be true; she believed it as in God himself.

One day I showed Malke a letter from Yosef in which he had written that he had looked at me through the telescope, and he had seen my girlfriend too. He realized this was Malke because of how lovingly she looked at me. He invited one of his good friends to have a look; this was his friend Georg, who was also a student, who was studying to be a lawyer. Georg had looked and had immediately fallen in love with Malke. He liked me too, but he saw her in a very different way; after all, I was already engaged, but Malke was something else. Malke immediately told her mother all about it, and her mother wrote her father in America; if it worked out, their daughter would have a lawyer for a husband. A lawyer, I explained, is a person who looks at the world and understands what's going on, which is how I understood it at the time. Malke didn't really grasp this. She would have preferred a doctor, which was something that everyone understood: a doctor earned thousands on the spot. But a lawyer—who knew what that was? But it didn't matter, it was clear that I had better luck than she.

Georg pelted Malke with letters. He wrote that Yosef would come in the summer, and he would come along too, so they could get better acquainted. Malke was in seventh heaven, and her mother heaped praises on me. I spent every evening with them, and Yosef and Georg watched us through their telescope. Eydl cleaned the house every day as if it were Pesach. She bought a new lamp because of the students in Moscow, and she put white covers on the cushions; the room felt renewed. Malke dressed up every day and flirted all the time, to be attractive. Georg wrote that he couldn't sleep at night because he was thinking about her. Malke could not wait for summer to come and bring the students with it. I had not yet decided what to tell her when the summer did come. I figured I would have Yosef and Georg suddenly go off to Italy. Meanwhile, Malke wrote Georg long philosophical letters, which I helped her with, because she didn't know what to say. It looked as if she had beautiful handwriting, which her mother boasted about to all the other housewives.

And so I survived the winter, writing letters; every miserable letter I received from my mother, I described to Yosef. I wrote him about the pain I felt. All of those letters, along with Malke's, I threw in the oven. I kept Georg's and Yosef's, though, and soon had an entire bundle of their handiwork. I altered the handwriting as best I could: Yosef's was one, Georg's another, and mine, still another. My shop lost a lot of business that winter and grew empty. Sheyne Gitl helped herself, the gentiles stole, and I didn't notice any of it; all I did was fantasize about Yosef the student. My aunts began to notice that I had strayed off the path and began to reproach me. I cried and complained about my wretched luck, and afterward, I poured my bitter heart out to Yosef.

9

Revenge

I could hardly wait for Pesach, when my mother was to come home. Once again I prepared her room carefully, just as I had the previous year, and I waited for Khatzkel the coachman to bring her. But when my mother arrived, she was only a shadow of her former self—an emaciated skeleton, the fire in her eyes extinguished. From her chest emerged a cacophony of rasping and wheezing. As soon as I saw her, I felt so wretched that I even forgot about Yosef. She looked at me angrily. Oh, I immediately understood why; Khatzkel must have told her that I had strayed off the path. Why would he say this to a miserable invalid? In this regard, Khatzkel was as good as a murderer.

My little brother arrived home from cheder. My mother called him in and questioned him about his studies, then told him to summon my grandfather. My grandfather soon came rushing in, not at all like an old man. He greeted her cordially, but she answered him only with a wheeze. She had my grandfather sit on a chair next to her bed, and my brother sat on another chair. My mother asked him to call me in too. I was very frightened of this summons; it felt like something terrible was going to happen. I slipped in quietly as a thief and stood next to my grandfather, not looking at my mother's clouded eyes or her sunken cheeks.

We all waited quietly for her to speak. She wheezed a few times and then beckoned for my brother to stand up. She took him by both hands and told him in a raspy voice: "My son, I beg you, with your old grandfather here as a witness: be a virtuous, pious Jew. Guard yourself from false companions. Observe Shabbes, and be honest. Have compassion for the poor. And do not forget your parents, who died before their time."

"Mama! What are you saying?" my brother exclaimed, "Only our father is dead; you are still alive! I don't want you to die! No, I won't let it happen!" He wept as he said these last words, and as soon as he stopped speaking, he began to choke on his tears. My mother wheezed even more, looking at him. I stood there, gnashing my teeth and clenching my fists, as I always did under duress. My heart had turned to stone, and I held back my own tears. My mother waited for my brother to calm down. She glanced at me and then turned to my grandfather and asked him why he had not noticed what was happening with me all winter: I had abandoned the store and was thinking only about my girlfriends and my books; I had neglected my duties. She turned to me. "Remember, my daughter," she said, "You don't have a mother any more. I already have one foot in the grave. How much more can I suffer? Three years is enough; I will never be well again. I feel that death is near. Pray for me, children, to have an easy death. I don't have any strength left to suffer."

I felt the tears well up; they rolled down my cheeks and fell to the ground. In the end, I was so overwrought that I began both crying and laughing uncontrollably. No one in those days recognized this as hysterics; they simply thought I had gone crazy. I screamed so loudly that the whole shtetl came running; everyone figured that my mother had already died. Indeed, when she heard my shrieking, my mother gave a kind of death rattle. My brother sat and cried silently. Someone brought in Khone the healer. He prescribed a bottle of almond milk for me and my mother and calmly went back home. Someone wrapped me in pillows, and I slept for a couple of hours.

When I woke up, it was already late at night. My brother was dozing over a book of Psalms; he had presumably been praying for my mother's health. My aunt Zlata and Basia-Reyzl were saying something to my mother, but I don't remember what. I went over to the cabinet, took out a siddur and also sat down to say Psalms—but I didn't simply recite them; I sang them with a melody, just as Oreh the melamed had taught me. When my brother heard me singing the Psalms so beautifully, he joined in and sang them with me. The women were soon mesmerized; our singing Psalms in the middle of the night was like a lullaby, and they dozed off. My mother sat and continued to wheeze. But by the time we had sung half of the Psalms, her eyes began to gleam once more as they had in the past. Her hollow cheeks grew rosy, and her figure straightened. She stood up tall and came over to us and kissed us both several times. "Children," she said, "I am kissing you perhaps for the last time. Remember this. Remember that your mother told you to follow a proper path in life." The more she spoke, the louder we tried to sing; we wanted God himself to hear us. My mother lay down to sleep. Despite our singing, we could hear an entire orchestra of sounds playing in her chest. This felt like a knife to the heart; we were angry that our Psalms had not helped. We threw aside our prayer books, lay down, and slept like children.

My aunt Zlata woke me early the next morning when she had to leave. My mother was sleeping quietly and peacefully, and my aunt said that she was doing better. Basia-Reyzl said that God had heard our Psalms. "Of course he did!" I thought to myself. "Why wouldn't he? God is good; we're the ones who are sinners." God had clearly heard an earnest prayer from deep in our hearts. Now that I knew what he liked, I thought, I would start reciting Psalms regularly. This was no chore! I had always loved the Psalms. They were such sweet prayers; it was not surprising that God loved them.

From then on, I sang Psalms whenever I had the time. The Psalms gave me a pleasure that is hard to describe; it was as if God were truly listening to me. My heart felt lighter, and my mind found some relief from all its heavy thoughts.

The holy holiday of Pesach arrived. No one joined us for our seder; my old uncle had gone to visit his children for the holiday, Sheyne-Gitl went to her father's, and we three were left to ourselves. I will remember that seder as long as I live. The house was bright, and the table was laid with all sorts of nice things. My brother sat at the head of the table, reclining on a large pillow; his face was as white as snow, but his eyes shone as my mother's used to do, his black hair gleaming. He sang the Haggadah aloud with a beautiful melody, though his eyes looked sad; he kept looking at the bed where my mother sat, pale as the wall, lost in her thoughts. I sang the Haggadah with my brother, and we did everything as it should be done. We ate more bitter herbs than matzo, and we counted off the plagues for Pharaoh, all two hundred and fifty as the sage Rabbi Akiva had laid out, because we hated Pharaoh as if he were a spider. I told my brother that, to all these plagues, I would have added our mother's illness; *that* would have been sufficient, I said. My mother laughed. We cheered up at her laughter, and we too began to laugh. It had been a long time since we had felt so happy.

While we ate, we made plans for the following year, when our mother would be healthy and sit with us at the seder, as in the past. I remembered that even back in the days when everything was good and our mother was well, she used to cry at our seders. Why was this, I wondered; things were so good for us then. If only we could say the same about today! My mother fell asleep, her chest wheezing so loudly that the walls trembled, and my brother and I felt sad again. Was there nothing that could help my mother? We had already tried everything, and nothing had helped, unless God were to throw a miracle down from heaven. And then I thought: why should God throw anything; did he not have an envoy to send? Here we were at Pesach, which meant that Elijah the prophet would come to our house when we opened the door to him. Couldn't Elijah bring a cure for my mother? After all, nothing is too hard for God. I told my brother what I was thinking. He approved of the doctor, but he didn't believe in the cure. He crushed all my hopes and made me angry.

"Just to spite you," I said, "God *will* send a cure through Elijah."

"Let us hope that he does," he said. "I would really want it. But I don't believe in miracles. You want to fantasize? May God make your fantasy come true."

"You'll see," I cried, "God *will* bring a miracle! It seems to me that you no longer even believe in God, for you to talk like this."

My brother smiled and said, "A woman doesn't understand anything about what God is. Mendl Karovitzer is truly right when he says that men are fully capable and women are something less. And you think that you know anything? Now hush, since God made you a girl; let others who are capable, and not like little children, speak of God's miracles."

I was very upset, but I decided not to respond this time, because I wanted tonight to be peaceful and quiet in our home. I wanted our revered visitor Elijah the prophet to be pleased, so he would leave behind a miraculous cure for my mother.

I could hardly wait to finish eating dinner. I ate a bit of the afikomen with some effort and hid the rest of it in my pocket, to give myself a bit of luck when we played our traditional Pesach games with nuts in the morning, and I poured a large glass of red wine for Elijah. The wine stood out nicely against the white tablecloth. In past years, my mother had set out a simple glass for him, but today I had chosen my mother's own pretty wine cup and placed it on a nice glass saucer, so Elijah would know that we were thinking of him. At the appropriate time, my brother signaled for me to open the door. I ran to the door, my heart beating like a hammer; I expected to see something extraordinary. I threw open the door and stood aside, holding onto the handle, to leave the threshold free for Elijah to step through. Despite my hopes, I couldn't see anything, but I did feel a breeze sweep through the room, and I thought Elijah must have flown in. But why couldn't I see him? It must be because I am sinful and unworthy of seeing him, I thought. I heard my brother recite the *Shfoykh khamoskho*, the invitation to God to pour out his wrath on the enemies of the Jews, and I trembled even more before the breeze that was still whirling through the room. Finally my brother called out for me to close the door, since he was finished; this meant that Elijah the prophet had left. I went to the threshold and looked outside.

How quiet and peaceful it was! All the windows were lit up, and there wasn't a soul in the street. The moon was shining bright, and I saw two faces in it—Moses the patriarch and Elijah the prophet, who must have had enough time to fly back up to the heavens already. I was envious of them both. If only I knew what a person was supposed to do, to be worthy of sitting in such brilliance in the world to come, then I would do it. "A sinful person like you would dare to think such things?" I thought to myself. "Who are you comparing yourself to? Look and be silent; you are not worthy of more."

Meanwhile, I heard a singing from afar. I listened a bit and then—aha! I caught a familiar motif. Ivan the gentile was singing my favorite song. His singing flowed throughout my body and glued me to my spot. I no longer saw any faces in the moon; I saw only a sea of brilliance and heard only the soft singing. Tears began to pour from my eyes. Quite unexpectedly, I saw Yosef standing before me, my confidant, my dear Yosef, who understood my joys and my suffering so well. I jumped down from the porch to go to him and tell him what I was thinking—but he had vanished. My heart dissolved with pain, and I thought I was going to pass out. I no longer heard any music. I remembered that it was already past midnight, and here I was standing all alone next to the Cold Shul, and I thought about the demons with the long tongues that Blumke had seen. I rushed back into the house and barred the door, as if someone were chasing me.

Back inside, I found my brother sleeping, sitting on his Pesach pillow, his head lying on his Haggadah. Elijah's cup stood there, full, just as I had poured it. My mother was sleeping, her chest wheezing. The candles were nearly out, and the shadows from the candlesticks were playing on the far wall. The lamp burned brightly, and in our broken mirror, I saw perhaps twenty eerie reflections. I began to tremble and went quietly to the table, where I laid my head down for a nap on my own Haggadah, like my brother. I closed my eyes and fell into a deep sleep. And so we remained until four in the morning.

My mother woke us up. As we were still rubbing our eyes, we could see that she was weeping. I asked her why, and she answered that she was thinking about our happy seder. Of course, she would want to survive another year and sit near us again, just like today. "But futile are my hopes, my dear children," she rasped, and she fell back on her pillow.

It was hard to revive my mother. Her sides, her chest, and her shoulders hurt. I laid a fire in the oven to warm up some plaster poultices for her. She lay as cold as ice; I was burning my fingers on the poultices, but she could not even feel them. Tears ran down my face. "My God!" I cried out, "What do you have against me? Why are you torturing me?" All my hopes were lost. I had waited futilely for Elijah's help. I won't believe in miracles any longer, I thought. It was foolish to be hopeful. I was so tired of suffering; I just wanted to die and be free of it all. What good was my life, if I felt so terrible? No—I would take my own life. I didn't care; let my mother cry as much as she wanted. If a person never had any luck, there was no reason to be alive. But how could I kill myself; where could I find poison? Then I remembered that common sulfur could work. All I needed was to do the deed, and I determined to do it that very day, the first day of Pesach, when I had some free time. I would first kiss my mother and my little brother, say viddui to confess my sins, burn Yosef's letters—and then I would die, peacefully. How good I would feel! I knew that a corpse could hear every word until the third scoop of ritual sand was dropped on it, so I would hear everyone weep over me.

When I warmed some water for a poultice, I also soaked two packets of sulfur in a glass. The sulfur water looked slimy. I hid it under my uncle's bed, and I felt completely calm.

In the meantime, my mother was doing better and had fallen asleep. The moon turned pale, the sky grew light. Dawn had arrived. I opened the door and sat on the porch; I wanted to see the sun rise for the last time. Gentiles went by, driving herds of cows to the fields. I asked one of them to braid me a wreath of blue cornflowers from the fields; I promised him a bagel in exchange. I wanted to poison myself while wearing a wreath on my head, just as a certain character in one of my novels had done. And to tell the truth, I simply wanted to have another look at the cornflowers, which I loved. The sun began to rise. I sat and bade farewell to it and to everything around me. I figured I would also go say goodbye to our beautiful river. And before I died, I would go have a nice drink of water from the priest's well. Then I would kiss my mother and my brother, drink up the bitter concoction—and be done.

Suddenly I heard a bell peal in the church, and then another. A fire!—I thought with a start. I looked around, but I couldn't see anything. Then I heard someone opening the windows and the doors at the priest's, and the farmhands and the servants were running around his courtyard. All at once, I saw that Akulina, the priest's cook, was coming over, bathed in tears; she told me to give her a pound of candles from our store. I began questioning her—Why was she crying? Why did she need candles so early in the day? Why were the church bells ringing? She answered in Russian, "*Nasha panienke pomerla!* Our young lady has died!"

The death of Sashke the *panienke*, the priest's daughter who had frightened my mother so badly three years back on April Fools' Day, was no great blow for me. I gave Akulina the candles and cried, "It serves her right, for what she did to my mother!"

Meanwhile, the church bell had roused all the neighbors; everyone was afraid there was a fire. I told them the news—the murderer Sashke, who had tricked my mother and made her sick, had dropped dead. All the neighbors danced with joy.

Sashke's illness had been hidden from everyone. She had gone away the previous year, to some distant, warm country, and a few weeks ago she had returned, as sallow as wax. The priest's servants said that she had consumption, but at home, everyone said that God had paid her back for my mother. She had been so healthy!—and now she was dead. Mera the seamstress said that Sashke had fallen ill because of a failed romance: she had fallen in love with a priest's farmhand from somewhere-or-other, and her father had not let her marry him. My aunt Zlata shouted that God himself had paid Sashke back for my mother. My mother got wind of the tumult on the street and went, all bent over, to the window, to ask everyone what the hubbub was about. The crowd spotted her at the window and began to clap their hands—*Serves her right; she was punished for you! You won't need your grave for a few dozen years; you'll live to enjoy your revenge. You'll see, from now on, you'll soon be healthy!* Listening to these words, my mother smiled and had a good chuckle. A small fire burned in her eyes, just like in the old days.

Looking at her smile and listening to everyone's words, I became merry. I ran into the house, grabbed the glass of poison, and poured it out into the wastewater, and I washed the glass as clean as if there had never been any poison in the world. My heart was full of hope. Once again I had something to look forward to, something to lean on. Thank God, Sashke had been punished for what she had done to my mother—may such an outcome come to everyone who does evil to Jews! I forgot completely about dying; I wanted only to live and hope for good times. That day I recited the entire Books of Psalms, and the walls resounded with my song.

In the afternoon, all the neighbors went to visit Sashke. The doors and windows were open for the viewing. Sashke lay on a sofa that had been draped in white and set in the middle of the room. She wore a white dress, with white stockings and white slippers, just like a bride. Her beautiful hair was plaited in a braid with white ribbon, and a wreath of white flowers lay atop her head. More garlands of flowers lay about, brought by the clergymen and their wives who had ridden in to pay their respects.

The gentiles sat around her, dressed in their expensive black clothes. Sashke herself was yellow as wax, her eyes closed; she lay like a block of wood. So this was what had become of the beautiful Sashke! No more her rosy cheeks, no more her chubby self; only her long braid remained. They all sat and looked at her silently, no tears to be seen—apparently the gentiles had hearts of stone. Could it really be that they didn't care when someone died? Sashke's three older sisters, ladies who together were perhaps a hundred years old, walked around like golems; they didn't cry, they didn't laugh . . . how on earth can someone not weep over putting such a beautiful girl as Sashke in the ground? It just goes to show that gentiles have no love for one another. What's a sister to a gentile? Nothing at all—she might as well be a stranger. Sashke died, so she'll be buried. What did you expect, among gentiles? We Jewish women, who had been so delighted that morning with Sashke's death, stood beside her with tears in our eyes as we saw what had become of her. I couldn't help it; my heart went out to her.

Some large candles were burning near Sashke's head, and a cleric stood and babbled something at her bedside. Smoke rose from some pungent incense burning on a little table . . . and watching the smoke rise, I wondered what had become of Sashke's soul. Perhaps she had already been reincarnated as a dog, or a pig? What would become of a sinful soul like hers? For my mother's suffering alone, she should be reincarnated seven times, each time in a different animal. But what would happen to her in the end? No doubt there was something written about this in our sacred texts. I decided to ask my brother if he knew.

Back at home, I found my brother sleeping. I woke him up, told him what I had seen at the priest's, and blurted out, "Where is Sashke's soul now? Do you know?"

He thought a minute and then answered, "Gentiles don't have souls; gentiles have spirits."

"What do you mean, spirits?"

"A spirit is a kind of ghost; there is a spirit in every gentile," my brother answered importantly.

"I figured that a gentile's soul would go into an animal, and then back into a gentile; that is, the souls of animals are the same as those of gentiles."

I said these words as a jest, as if I didn't believe it myself, because I didn't want him to laugh at me. Compared to my brother, I had fallen far behind in my education, so I didn't want to say what I thought. But this time my brother agreed that it might be correct that the souls of gentiles and animals were the same. I was gratified and decided that Sashke's soul had definitely gone into a pig. In my opinion, she had not merited any better.

Sashke had already lain in the ground next to the church for a couple of weeks; grass was starting to sprout on her grave. And my mother kept wheezing. I came to regret that I was still alive, but I could take care of that whenever I wanted—there was no shortage of sulfur. I was now scared of *khibut-hakever*, however, which my brother had told me about at length. This was a sort of divine punishment that a new corpse is put through inside the grave by the angels of death, a preliminary expiation of sins involving shaking and beating the newly deceased. On the one hand, I figured I could be thrown from one end of the world to the other, and would I be any worse off than I already was? But I decided it was better to suffer here, where I could atone for my sins.

Meanwhile, the situation at home had deteriorated. Sheyne-Gitl had been dismissed, and I had to run the house and the store as well as tend to my mother. I was so tired I couldn't even make the challah for Shabbes. My mother woke me one Friday at dawn to have me knead the dough. I stood next to her bed, my feet bare and my arms uncovered; I held a pitcher of water in one hand, and with the other I held on to a chair so I wouldn't fall down, because my eyes were still glued shut. I was dying to go to sleep. The pitcher slipped from my hand, and water gushed into the kneading trough, turning the dough into soup. My mother got angry and began hitting my hands. She yelled that I was a disaster, that God had punished her with everything; he hadn't even given her proper children! I began to cry. I knew that my mother was right, but what could I do? I was so weary. In the end, my aunt Zlata came and made the challah. The next Friday, we went through the same ordeal.

One day, when I went to her room to look for something, I found a large piece of linen, fine as silk and white as snow.

"Mama," I asked, "what kind of linen is this?"

She answered, "These are my eternal clothes, my daughter. I want to lie in a real linen shroud. There's no doubt I will die soon, and where would you get a nice shroud here in Bulin?"

I threw down the linen and ran out, shouting that I was going to burn the material. I ran to the shul, opened the Holy Ark, and had a good cry there. The little boys who were studying in the shul burst into tears. From there I ran to my grandfather's house. My grandfather calmed me down and told me that even someone who prepared a shroud could live for a hundred years. He promised that he would make an announcement in both shuls the next day to ask everyone to pray for my mother, and God would no doubt help. With these reassurances, I composed myself and went home.

I found my mother sleeping and my brother sitting next to her with a prayer book. He told me that my mother had cried a long time before she fell asleep. The next day was Thursday, and they prayed for her in both shuls at the afternoon service. And so we passed another couple of weeks in sorrow and pain.

We made it to Erev Shavuos, in late spring. That day, my mother sent for my grandfather and my uncles and cousins while I was busy in the store. When they arrived, she told them that she wanted to say viddui, her confession before dying. They tried to dissuade her, but in the end they agreed. The shammes brought a small book of prayers for the dying and the dead, the *Mayver-yabek*, and he said some specific words from it, which my mother repeated after him. My brother stood on the other side of the door and wept. When I realized what was happening, I ran in like a maniac and began yelling at the shammes to go away—what was he doing here? I didn't want him to shorten my mother's life! My grandfather steered me into the kitchen and persuaded me that they were doing this as a kind of therapeutic treatment. My brother and I sat on the porch and cried bitter tears; the women walking by sighed when they looked at us. We could hardly wait for everyone to leave.

Finally we went back in the house. My mother was weeping quietly, reciting something from the women's prayer book. The *Mayver-yabek* lay on the table. I snatched it up without my mother seeing and threw it into the oven, and I cooled my heart, watching it burn.

10

May Her Memory Be a Blessing

The morning after Shavuos, my aunt Zlata told me to write my grandmother and tell her to come. My mother didn't know about the letter. She was feeling a bit better, but on the fifth day after the holiday, she seemed withdrawn the entire day, her face dark. At three in the afternoon, she called together her aunts and cousins and told them she was dying. She implored my aunt Zlata to watch over my brother and me until my grandmother and my uncles could decide what to do with us, and she told my aunt to rely on them entirely. She wanted her children to remain in the area, since she was afraid we would lose our Jewish way of life in the big city. She was especially afraid on my brother's behalf. As for me, she said that it would be best if I were married off sooner rather than later. They should find me a refined young man and give me the house for the dowry. This was my mother's last will and testament.

They called my brother and me in to her. My mother embraced us both and held us for some minutes, until she suddenly fell back on the bed. She wheezed for a few minutes, and then she lay still. Basia-Reyzl held a feather to her nose. We heard one more gasp, and then the feather stopped moving—she had fallen into her eternal sleep. "Your mother is no more, children!" my aunt Zlata cried. We all began to howl. . . .

Someone laid my mother on the floor. They lit candles and covered her with a black cloth. The entire shtetl soon knew that my mother had died, and our house was besieged with visitors; there was hardly room to go in or out. The women sat on the floor around her and wailed. Moyshke the shammes bustled about nervously. The coattails of his kapote were caught up in his belt, and he wrung his hands and bobbed his head as if he didn't know what to do first. My grandfather told him they should dig a grave in a place of honor in the new cemetery, uphill. Moyshke nodded so vigorously that the knots in his hair flew in all directions. Khana Motls and Rokhl Eliakims stood next to the table, hastily sewing a shroud from the large piece of linen I had wanted to burn. Rokhl showered praise on the material, how fine it was and how pure, and how appropriate for my mother, who had lived like a *tsaddik* and died like one too.

I sat on the floor near my mother's head and tore bits of flesh from my hands until they ran with blood. I wept, too, but more quietly than I was supposed to. I was supposed to scream, to beg, to talk to my mother—this was the last time I could speak to her.

But I was wretched, and I couldn't speak. Why was everybody else so clever? What pearls flowed from their mouths! I'm not even talking about my aunts; casual acquaintances spoke with a fervor that might have melted stones, and they all begged my mother to entreat God for my brother and me. Why did they need to ask? I thought. Did she not know? Who else would she pray for, if not us? But no doubt it was right to remind her. My aunt Zlata's entreaties were the most painful for me; she spoke fluently and at length. She appealed to my mother for us, for herself and her children, for my old grandmother who now had to be our mother, for my mother's brothers and sister, who had to bring us up, and for good measure, for all the aunts and their children too. Then she began to convey greetings to those in the world to come, to the grandmother and the aunts who had raised my mother; she told her what to say to them when she met them in Paradise. Oh, they would all surely come to meet her! The whole time, Zlata screamed in my mother's ear that she shouldn't forget her children, and everyone dissolved in tears. Even Khodosia, the gentile water carrier, who understood Yiddish well, stood there and cried. I was the only one who sat like a piece of wood.

"Why are you not speaking? Do you have nothing to say to your mother?" Khaye-Beyla asked me quietly. I answered that I couldn't speak, that my heart had turned to stone. Khaye-Beyla whispered in Khaye-Ita's ear that I could speak well enough with my friends, yet I didn't know what to say to my own mother. Khaye-Ita answered that in her opinion, I was altogether pleased to be free of her; my mother had gotten to be odious to me, with her illness. I drew a little closer to my mother and waited for a miracle, for my mother to tell Khaye-Ita off and say she was lying. But my mother lay there and didn't move a muscle.

Meanwhile Khana and Rokhl had finished making the shroud. "Women, get up!" Moyshke the shammes cried. "It is time to wash the corpse!" We all stood up. Two women carried in a plank and laid it on chairs, and my mother was lifted onto it. Someone brought in two buckets of water. I was standing at my mother's head so I could see what they were doing. When they uncovered her face, I began to shriek. Our neighbor Malke-Rokhl could hardly drag me out into the next room. She said I wasn't allowed to be with my mother just then. I screamed for her to let me go, but to no avail. She let me back in after my mother was laid out in the fine, pure shroud, with a white cloth wrapped around her head. Her face looked as black as coal against the cloth. When I saw her, I screamed and howled and tore the hair from my head, with everyone looking at me and moaning.

Soon the shammes cried out again, and the women told me I should beg my mother to forgive me for everything that I had done to sin against her. Again I was distressed; what should I say to her? She herself knew that I had not sinned against her. They all saw how she had kissed me before she died; she must have forgiven me everything already. I was unable to speak; others would have to do the talking for me. My aunt Zlata approached my mother and argued fervently on my behalf for some time. Then someone led in my brother, who had been sitting in the garden crying. My aunt Tobe asked my mother to forgive him too. My grandmother the rebbetzin, who had been standing apart this whole time because she was afraid of the dead, now approached; she stood next to my mother and trembled like a leaf. After her came the neighbors and good friends, and this all lasted a long time, because who in our shtetl was not a neighbor, and who is not a good friend to someone who has died?

The shammes gave another cry. There was a commotion, and the women were swept outside, me along with them. The men went in, laid my mother on a litter, and carried her out of the house. The crowd of women wailed so loudly that the gentiles nearby started weeping too. My brother and I held hands, both crying "Mama!" The men carried our mother to the shul, and afterward, to her eternal resting place in the cemetery. My aunt Zlata walked along through the streets, arguing aloud the entire time as if from a book. She was speaking to God now, asking him questions and answering them herself, all the while justifying God's actions. The boys from the shammes's cheder walked along, singing verses of Psalms. The shammes rattled his collection box and called out in

Hebrew, "*Tzedakah tatzil mimavet!* Charity saves from death!"

We reached the cemetery, where a deep, dark grave had already been dug. I started to tremble. This is where they would put my mother? To think of her all alone in such a cold, gloomy place; my beautiful, clever mother, covered with soil. And who would do the job? Zalmen the carpenter, whom my mother always laughed at, because one could readily see by his own sukkah how incompetent he was. But nevertheless, so it was. Someone reminded my mother not to forget her own name, Sarah, when she arrived in the world to come. I had no doubt she would remember: when praying, she had always said our matriarch Sarah's name in a loud voice, and she had specifically asked Oreh the melamed to teach me the verses from scripture with my own name. Three times she was reminded not to forget her name, and her emaciated frame was lowered with ropes deep into the grave on some boards, along with a little sack of soil from the Holy Land. Her bones had grown stiff even while she had lain on the large featherbed back at home, and now she lay there, meekly. Someone approached me, cut my jacket over my heart, and told me to wear it like that for an entire year. Zalmen began to throw in soil, one shovel after the other, and before long a mound covered the grave—my mother lay under a heavy little mountain. My little brother said kaddish in a loud voice. How envious I was of him! There was good reason for my mother to be delighted with him, but what kind of parental pride would she have for me in the world to come? For the first time in my life, I felt unlucky to have been born a girl. A boy may indeed be cherished by his parents: he is worthy of love just for the mitzvah of saying the mourner's prayer, which my brother would continue to do three times a day for the next eleven months. My mother would surely be all right, lying in her grave, having left behind such a son to say kaddish for her.

I felt somewhat reassured with this thought and let myself be taken home with the rest of the women. Along the way, they talked about my mother's piety and her many acts of charity. They wondered that she had not cut off her hair before she died, but she had said that she didn't want to fool God: she would arrive in the world to come just as she had been here. Then they chatted about what would become of my brother and me after my grandmother arrived. Someone mentioned some young Talmud scholar who wanted to marry me. No one spoke to me or paid any attention to me. In a big city, good friends would walk by a mourner's side and comfort her; they'd take her by the hand and accompany her home. It was not like that in our shtetl. Here, no one visited a mourner until the third day, even if she might go crazy in the meantime.

My brother did not have to sit shiva because he was not yet thirteen, and my mother's mother and her brothers and sister were still hundreds of miles away, so as the only principal mourner, I sat by myself on the floor, feeling as if I had been severed from the world. The good, dear Basia-Reyzl brought us the round food that was traditional after a burial: two eggs dipped in ash, with a string of bagels. Khodosia, the gentile water carrier, tidied up the room a bit and carried out my mother's soiled clothes. I gave her a bagel for this. She sat down next to me to comfort me and told me that her mother had also died. She was left an orphan too, but poorer than I, and all alone. This is how she came to be married at eighteen to Daniel the thief, who now had several children by her, and even though he beat her a couple of times a week, she was nonetheless content—at least she wasn't alone. "Don't worry," she consoled me, "You too will get married and you won't be alone. Just pray to God for a good husband." She kept talking in this vein until she had finished her bagel, which she ate in tiny bites. Then she crossed herself, said good night, and left.

My brother lit the small lamp and went to bed. I remained sitting on the ground. The broken mirror had been covered with my mother's black cashmere shawl. The windows were open, and the moon shone in through the window right in my face. I stared at the moon, lost in my thoughts. Where was my mother's soul now? Was it in Paradise, I wondered, among all the holy souls, or perhaps in the seventh level of heaven? I wasn't at all concerned about hell—my mother was a pure soul, virtuous and pious. She must already be in Paradise. But could she still feel her body in its grave? How could anyone feel all right in a cold, dark grave, under a mound of earth? The worms must already be eating her, I thought, and here I am, sitting in the light. Tears ran down my cheeks. I feel you, dear Mama, how heavy the earth must be, and how you must be so cramped, and cold, but I cannot help you. If your soul is in Paradise, I wondered, how can your body be doing so badly? I couldn't comprehend this at all. Did the body have any connection to the soul after death? I thought about this for a long time, until I decided that a girl was just not supposed to think about such things. But my heart ached for my mother, and I fell asleep, still sitting on the ground.

The next morning, Basia-Reyzl again brought me food. I read the Book of Job all day. In the evening, Khodosia the water carrier came again and sat with me a bit. Today she was in a completely different mood, not nearly as sanguine as she had been the day before. She complained about her bitter luck: Daniel had beaten her nearly to death today. Her whole body was covered in bruises. She told me that an orphan could not be happy, that everyone was mean to her. If she had not been an orphan, would Daniel have had the audacity to beat her? No, he beat her precisely because he knew that she had no one to defend her. "You'll also be like this with your husband someday," she told me as she left.

After her, my friends Malke and Merke came to call on me. We didn't speak; they simply sat with me for a couple of hours. The three of us cried, and they left without even saying good night. What could they say? It wasn't appropriate to chat about the things we usually talked about, and they couldn't console me, so they remained silent. But their tears spoke volumes.

The next day, the women finally started to visit, and the door didn't close all day. They talked and talked, they heaped praise on my mother, they pitied us, they sighed and groaned over me. Their pity made my heart ache.

Friday morning brought my poor grandmother. She stepped down from the coach as erect and proud and beautiful as ever, but when she came into the house and saw me sitting on the floor, she crumpled, and her hands began to shake. My aunt Zlata came running in soon after, and they fell into each other's arms and began to carry on. My grandmother could speak well, too, when she had to, and it felt to me as if my mother were still lying on the ground, and they were mourning over her all over again. Then my brother came in, and my grandmother cried out fervently, "God! Give me the strength to raise my daughter's children!" When she finished her entreaties, she sat down on the floor beside me.

On Shabbes, the house was again full of women all day. My grandmother told everyone that she had not yet decided what she would do with us; she would have to consult her children. In the days that followed, my grandfather came with a minyan to pray every day, my brother said kaddish, and the tears flowed down my grandmother's face.

11

Farewell to My Home

An entire month went by. Matchmakers began to show up at our house with potential bridegrooms, and they were real gems, each one better than the last. Many of them didn't even know me personally, but they knew my pedigree and my reputation, and they knew I was clever enough to run a store. My grandmother bargained with the matchmakers and made all kinds of plans without saying a word to me. When I heard about this, I was beside myself. Was she serious? Could they really marry me off to a simple yeshiva boy? Did they expect me to stay in our dismal, ignorant shtetl and be a shopkeeper all my life? What about my own hopes and plans?

Meanwhile, I had stopped thinking about Yosef. I didn't actually forget him, but I didn't write him any more letters, because Malke had stopped believing in him. A local boy named Aharon, Khayim-Dovid's only son, who came by frequently to visit my brother, had opened her eyes. Malke had told him the whole story, and when she showed him some of the letters, he really made fun of her. He pointed out that the letters were in my handwriting and said that I had made the entire thing up: Yosef and Georg didn't exist. Malke was furious. How could I have duped her? Aharon calmed her down and told her to keep quiet, because otherwise everyone would laugh at her, and it would cause trouble for me. Malke told her mother, and the two of them were miserable; they were outraged at having been deceived by a child like me. Mera the seamstress was completely astonished. Malke came running over to my house and wanted to tear me to shreds. I was not scared; I freely admitted that I had simply wanted to play a trick on her, and there was nothing more to it. But I was ashamed to look her mother in the eye. I was also embarrassed in front of Aharon, and I hated him with every bone in my body.

And so Yosef vanished like a dream. In my heart, however, he lived on just as before, and I still wrote him little notes. I complained to him especially when I heard someone talking about arranging a marriage for me; I implored him to take me away to a big city. I wanted to study and live among educated people. If I stayed here in Bulin, they would marry me off to some crass young man who would do nothing but loaf around, and I would forever be a shopkeeper and have a miserable life, without any time to myself. "No, Yosef!" I wrote to him, "I don't want that kind of life; I want to live like you!" But Yosef, that villain, kept as silent as a wall.

Day by day, things began to feel a bit calmer at home. One day my grandmother told me they were arranging a magnificent match for me, with a fellow from a small shtetl. The prospect was a distinguished scholar, and after the wedding he would go off to study in the renowned Lithuanian city of Kovno. "In the meantime," she said, "you'll support him from the store. Afterward, with God's help, you'll have a rabbi for a husband, which would be quite suitable for you. Your mother valued Torah scholarship, and so should you. By the way, your grandfather agrees."

I heard her out and replied that I wouldn't say anything against the plan until I had seen the fellow, but that I was not in a hurry to get married. Who got married at fourteen in those days? But my grandmother had thought it through, and she explained that by the time the engagement contract went through, I would be fifteen, and at the wedding I would be sixteen; and by sixteen, one wasn't considered too young to be married. I began to entertain the idea. On the one hand, I was tempted. I was pleased with the notion of being a bride; I'd have new clothes made, and a plush coat, and I'd get a fancy new hat with flowers. And the wedding itself would be joyful, with music and dancing. Everyone would be jealous and feel honored to sit next to me. My grandfather would put on his kittel and bless me at the chuppah, just as he did at Yom Kippur. And my aunt might come again from Rishelevsk, dressed in silk, and perhaps she would even bring a silk dress for me too. My grandmother would busy herself with the waiters, and I would wear a white dress with a long train; I had never seen one, but I knew about them from my books. I would hold flowers and my heart would be full, seeing how excited everyone was because of me. As for the bridegroom, I didn't think about him at all. What did I care who he was? He certainly wouldn't be anything like Yosef, so he might as well be anybody.

I was almost ready to agree to the match when I thought about my mother. A chill went through my bones. What has become of you, my beautiful, dear mother? Here I am having fun, and you are lying in the ground!

After the fall holidays, my grandmother went back to Rishelevsk to consult with my uncles about what to do with my brother and me. In the meantime, we lived by ourselves all winter. My brother was a good student and could write well, so by now there was no melamed in our shtetl who could teach him; he would have to be sent away somewhere to study. I wrote to my grandmother about this and waited for an answer.

Meanwhile, I was preoccupied with the store. Because I sold goods on credit, I didn't have much cash to buy merchandise. I was used to people borrowing money from us, but in the end, I had to resort to borrowing too. Although I had good credit, I hated borrowing more than anything. I wouldn't want to go through that again. My aunts said that I was overwhelmed; they thought I was giving money to my friends. Malke especially got what she wanted from me, they said. My heart did break for her; the poor thing was fighting with everyone. I would have given her something if I had anything to give. Instead, I remained silent and wished I were dead.

Finally I got some unexpectedly happy news—my uncles had decided to bring us to Rishelevsk. What joy! I would no longer have to deal with all the housewives or suffer from the gentile thieves, or from Stepan the drunkard, who came banging at my window in the middle of the night. In short, in my new life in the city, I would be free of all my problems. I was delighted, and the girls and boys in Bulin were jealous. But my grandfather was not pleased. I dismissed his concern, because I knew that he wasn't thinking about me; he was worried about my brother losing his Jewish identity. However, what happened next made my grandfather's concern for my brother moot: my grandfather took ill, lay in bed for five days, and died suddenly in the middle of the night.

I simply can't describe the enormous effect his death had in the shtetl. He had been a rabbi in Bulin for thirty-three years; he was an institution. Everyone wept from the bottom of their hearts. When I hurried over in the morning, his house was already full of men; the only other women there were my grandmother, my grandfather's poor, sickly daughter, and his one remaining daughter-in-law. They didn't let any other women in; in fact, my aunts had to argue for me too. I sat next to them on the floor and wept. My grandmother the rebbetzin trembled before my dead grandfather, as if he were going to call her away to the next world too; she sat at a distance and wailed.

A few hours later, they carried my grandfather into the shul. The entire congregation sat on the floor, weeping, and the *shoykhet*, our ritual slaughterer, delivered the eulogy. I remember that I took a lot of pride in that eulogy. I listened with a sad, vain expression, like a princess whose father had been dethroned. What I didn't realize was that this marked the end of our family's elevated position of respectability: my handsome grandfather with his bushy eyebrows and his fiery eyes was no more, and there was no longer anyone to bless us on Yom Kippur. "The beauty is gone from your head, children," the *shoykhet* told us; "There is no one left in your family who is such a *tsaddik* as he!" And all of us, my grandfather's children, wept and wept.

The winter passed. After Pesach, my grandmother came back to Bulin with a completely different plan: she would still take me with her to Rishelevsk, but she would send my little brother to the famous yeshiva in Mir so he would remain deeply immersed in Jewish life. My poor brother was miserable. I was like a mother to him; he didn't want to be separated from me, and he didn't want to be alone. He was also scared to leave Bulin. He had never spent even a single night away from home, and now all of a sudden he was supposed to go far away and adjust to being with strangers. I was distraught, and my heart ached for him. I knew that he was a delicate child; in a strange place, who would keep an eye on him? My grandmother laughed at us both. She said that she herself would take him, and she would rent him a nice apartment with room and board, and by no means would he have to have "eating days" like other yeshiva boys, who had to eat with a different family every day of the week. Despite her reassurances, I was not pleased. Over the years, there had been times when I was sick of my brother, and times when I thought I hated him, but now I realized more than ever how dear he was to me.

My grandmother took matters into her own hands and began to get my brother ready for the journey. She bought him clothes and a year's worth of all kinds of supplies. She hired Fayvke the Shlimazel as a coachman, and on a nice, bright day, they left for the Mir Yeshiva. My brother sobbed when we parted. Fayvke didn't linger; he gave a shout to his white horse and they were off, my brother still crying in the coach. I sat on the porch and wept. I stayed there until Fayvke's horse turned onto a different street and they disappeared from view. When I went back inside, I thought I was going to pass out. One of the beds was bare, since my brother had taken the bedding, and the house felt barren. I didn't know what to do with myself, and I kept running out into the street, crying.

In a few days, my grandmother returned and said that she had settled my brother like the child of a lord; he wouldn't want for anything. And then she began to get ready to depart with me. She sold all of our things from the store and the house to our neighbor, who also leased the house with the intention of turning it into a store. I was pleased that a neighbor would remain in our house, and I hoped that he would grow rich. When my grandmother sold the chest of drawers, she cried; she had bought it for my mother as a wedding present. She told me how much it had cost, how beautiful it was, and how my mother had filled it with linen blouses. With every item, my grandmother had a story to tell about how she had raised my mother and gotten her married. Tears streamed down her wrinkled cheeks. She did not sell my mother's silk dress; she kept that for me, along with the linen blouses, which my mother had sewn herself. "Set these aside, my child," she said. "Keep them to remember you had a mother who had a golden touch."

As I took everything out of the chest, I came across a packet of letters that my mother had accumulated. In them was described everything from her bitter life to her love for us; there were letters of consolation from her brothers, affectionate letters from her sister, and letters from my father. I chose the most interesting and threw the rest in the oven. Yosef's letters also went into the oven—I didn't want to keep them or even think about them. I wanted to put an end to my old life and start afresh, and I wanted to put all my foolishness behind me. Enough of my dreaming, enough living with fantasies; I wanted to face life with my eyes wide open. In the meantime, though—the sooner I could get out of here, the better. I didn't want to look at the muddy walls of our house any longer, or tread on the ground that was soaked with my tears.

Early on a Monday, I got up with the sun and went off to the river. The silent water reflected the sun in a variety of colors; I had never seen it so beautiful. Could it really be that I would never see our river again? How I would miss it! I walked home, step by step, looking back until it was out of sight.

Later I went with my grandmother to the cemetery to say farewell to my mother. I won't attempt to describe the scene that took place there. I can only say that the shammes cried himself out, watching us. My mother's grave had a heavy stone lying on it, and the stone was already overgrown with grass.

When we got back home, the coachman had packed our things into his wagon, and the entire shtetl had gathered by our house. My aunts wailed, looking at me and my old grandmother and the empty house. The coachman had already harnessed his horse and told us to get in, and then the tears really started to flow. I took my leave of everyone, and everyone gave me dozens of blessings for the journey. Our neighbors Khaye-Ita, Malke-Rokhl, and Khaye-Beyla were bathed in tears, and my girlfriends, Merke and

Malke, held me tight. But all things come to an end, and my grandmother was already sitting in the coach. I said goodbye for the last time, and I climbed in too.

The coachman gave his horse a lash, and in a few minutes, they had all vanished from sight. At the outskirts of the shtetl, I turned to look back once more, but all I could see was the spire of the church. Adieu, my dear old home; farewell to my childhood! I did not have good years there, but even so, I felt sad; those years would never come back. My heart began to pound—where was I going? My old world had disappeared, but I could not yet see the new one. What would I encounter in the big, new world? Could it possibly be as bad as the old? Who could tell?

Epilogue

Half a year after my grandmother took my brother to the Mir Yeshiva, he fell ill. The doctors could not diagnose his illness. He pined for Bulin and his cheder friends, and he particularly longed for his rebbe, who had always discussed divine matters with him. In the end, he simply wasted away. He had always been a delicate child, and he was not strong enough to handle all of the great changes that took place during his short life. He returned to Bulin and died in our shtetl, my brother Yitzhak, my little Itske. His memory will live forever in my heart.

I did not adjust quickly to my new life in Rishelevsk either. My former home was always on my mind, whether I was looking at the fine, broad streets of the city, or strolling along its lovely boulevards, or sitting in one of its magnificent theaters. I kept thinking about the simple men and women who were so dear to me back home.

When I visited Bulin recently, my emotions were a jumble; it felt as if I were calling on a sick relative. The closer I got, the stranger and more unrecognizable everything seemed. Our old home was no longer even there; my uncle had built a dazzling new one in its place. How I wanted to visit our old house, where I was born, where I spent my childhood, and where I knew and loved every wooden beam! My mother used to say that our roof leaked because it was infected with our tears. But the old house was gone, as if it had never even existed.

Many of my old acquaintances were also gone. Our neighbors Khaye-Ita and Malke-Rokhl had died, and our dear boarder Basia-Reyzl, who had lived with us for so many years, was old and blind; she didn't recognize me or even know who I was. But her husband, my old teacher Mikhoel the melamed, expounded at length just like in the old days. He was very stooped over, but this didn't affect his ability to talk.

I went to the cemetery with my aunts to visit the graves of my mother, my brother, and my grandfather. Even strangers came to pour out their hearts to these graves. Just as people had been accustomed to coming to my grandfather throughout their lives to settle their quarrels and administer justice, so they continued to come to him after his death. On the day we visited the cemetery, a small group of women was standing at his gravestone, crying, *Rabbi, don't forget us; may your merits in heaven protect us!* When the women noticed my aunts and me, they moved away from his grave. We approached his stone proudly, just as we used to go to him every year on Yom Kippur. I stood at his grave, tears pouring from my eyes.

My aunts saw that I was not asking my grandfather for anything, so they entreated him on my behalf. The other women looked at me as if I were crazy: to come here from the end of the world to visit the grave of a beloved grandfather, a grandfather who was a *tsaddik* no less, and then to remain silent and not even speak a single word!—apparently something happens to people when they move to the big city. I wondered if my grandfather understood me in my silence.

Back in the shtetl, everything seemed turned upside-down. The wealthy had become poor, and the simple had raised themselves up and become respectable. The old aristocratic class, which my family had belonged to, was gone.

It was painful to witness the demise of my family, which had at one time illuminated the entire shtetl and the surrounding region with its splendor. At first, I consoled myself with the fact that my relatives still had their pride and their sense of family honor; had we not had that spirit, we would have not survived in today's world. But later, when I observed them myself, they seemed like shadows of their former selves. My heart hurt, and I had to escape; I couldn't bear to witness their suffering. My aunt Zlata cried and begged me to stay another few days, because she hadn't finished telling me about her many problems.

Whom could she tell, if not me, one of her own kin? But I already understood her problems all too well.

I took leave of my pedigreed relatives as they came to see me off. I bade farewell to our yard with its handsome new house, and I consoled myself that at least it had stayed in my aunt's hands and didn't belong to some stranger. I left behind the Cold Shul and our pretty stream. At the outskirts of the shtetl, I thought to say goodbye to our woods, but I saw that it had already been chopped down. Such a beautiful forest! Now it looked as if it had never been there. As I traveled on and lost sight of the shtetl, I felt as if my heart were breaking. I would never come again, I thought. At the same time, I felt something pulling me back. But what was left for me here?

And then I remembered one thing that would forever bind me to this place: the graves of my mother, my brother, and my grandfather. As I traveled the winding road farther and farther away from Bulin, I thought about the gravestones that were so precious to me, and I felt at peace. I knew that I would always return to visit them, no matter how far away I was. As for the shtetl of my youth, I know now that I will never find it again. As time goes on, it will keep changing, and every time I come back, it will seem even more foreign. I console myself with one thing, though, that I have written down these memories, the good with the bad. My old shtetl is as vivid in these pages as it was long ago in my childhood years.

Translator's Afterword

When *My Childhood Years* was published in serialized form in 1905 and then in book form in 1909, it was a hit, not only with ordinary readers but also with the literati. Feygenberg's story, at times very funny, at times full of pathos, was a clear-eyed description of her narrator's young life, with three-dimensional, flawed characters and compelling descriptions of the details of everyday shtetl life. Feygenberg's portrayal of the shtetl, unlike that of the *klasikers*, was grounded in reality, and that reality evoked a certain kind of nostalgia for its citified readers. As Noakh Prilutski wrote in a glowing contemporaneous review of the 1909 book form of *My Childhood Years*: "The old familiar Jewish shtetl is presented as it really was: not with a satirical eye or with humor, not with the angst of someone disgusted by it, not with the pain of a sufferer, not with the mud and the prayer halls; it is not [Mendele's fictitious] Glupsk and not [Sholem Aleichem's fictitious] Kasrilevke—in short, seen not from a negative, but from a positive perspective; from the inside, presented as a beloved, treasured, sweet home."[1]

The success of *My Childhood Years* changed Rokhl Feygenberg's life. She had been working as a seamstress in Odesa to suit her socialist sympathies, but she had never shaken her childhood yearning for an education; her fervent dream was to become a writer. Through their correspondence, her editor Shaul Ginzburg took an interest. He knew that this early literary endeavor, while promising in so young a writer, was no guarantee of a talent that would last to maturity. He decided to sponsor Feygenberg, summoned her to Saint Petersburg—she had a certificate as a seamstress that allowed her the right of residence there—and paid her to write while she studied. Ginzburg's sponsorship paid off, as he reflected decades later: "I can say with great satisfaction that the hopes I laid on her literary future did indeed come to pass. Her talent developed and strengthened. She became a great, prolific writer."[2]

Rokhl Feygenberg's Early Years as a Writer

When Feygenberg accepted Shaul Ginzburg's sponsorship and moved from Odesa to Saint Petersburg following the 1905 publication of *My Childhood Years*, it would have been as big a shift for the twenty-year-old as her upheaval had been when she had moved from Lyuban to Odesa after her mother had died. Odesa was modern and cosmopolitan, but it was in the Pale, and more than one-third of its population was Jewish.[3] By comparison, Saint Petersburg, one thousand miles to the north on the Baltic Sea, was the capital of the Russian heartland and boasted about 1.2 million residents, of which only about 17,000, or less than two percent, were Jewish. Furthermore, unlike Lyuban and unlike Odesa, the Jews of Saint Petersburg were a rarefied set of wealthy merchants, intellectuals, and literati; there were no sweatshops and no pogroms in Saint Petersburg. They were also much more Russified; in 1897, roughly a third of its Jewish residents spoke Russian as their native tongue.[4]

For Feygenberg, the timing was fortuitous. Universities were still closed to women in Russia, but the "Higher Courses for Women" that had been established in the 1870s functioned as their equivalents, even though the women who studied in these institutions were not granted the same advantages awarded to their male counterparts; they were classified as "auditors" rather than "students" and therefore denied privileges like the right of residence. But following the Russian Revolution of 1905, spurred by a wake of public activism, the educational opportunities for women expanded enormously; the number of women enrolled in the Higher Courses for Women across Russia more than doubled during 1906–8 alone.[5]

When she arrived in Saint Petersburg, Feygenberg spent about two and a half years studying privately to complete the equivalent of seven years in a Russian gymnasium (high school), following which Ginzburg secured a two-year scholarship for her to study history and literature in the Higher Courses for Women.[6] Meanwhile, he paid her as a writer, and between 1906 and 1908, when Ginzburg withdrew from publishing *Der fraynd*, Feygenberg published six stories in the paper while also pursuing her studies.

Feygenberg's intellectual and personal development must have undergone a huge expansion during this period of her life. Her proletarian sympathies may have been awakened in her Odesa years, but she never again worked with her hands. In her Higher Courses for Women, fewer than five percent of the students were Jewish, and these were primarily assimilated Jews.[7] Unlike them, Feygenberg continued her religious practice—her friends called her "rebbetzin"—and despite being ensconced in an intellectual environment, she cast her own critical and ironic eye on the world around her. In a piece she wrote years later for the newspaper *Der moment*, she recalled two of her good friends from her days in Saint Petersburg.[8] One was another "auditor" who lived in an apartment in the same house as Feygenberg; she was a young Jewish woman who was the daughter of a rich timber merchant from the Baltics. This friend had fallen in love with a Russian student and was ready to convert on the spot for him; her boyfriend Sergei, however, was a freethinker who had renounced Christianity. Sergei was studying philosophy, and having taken on a project of researching the origins of religions of different peoples, he was fascinated with Feygenberg and constantly asked her to provide details of her religious practice, assiduously recording her answers in a little notebook he always carried. The girlfriend, who had grown up in an assimilated family and had no experience of Jewish practice, was forever trying to tempt Feygenberg away from her own observance, as when she tried to get Feygenberg to sample pork, or by offering food and milk while Feygenberg was suffering from a headache while fasting for Yom Kippur. Feygenberg, who in chapter 2 of *My Childhood Years* had her narrator speak of losing her faith, tried to explain to her friends why she continued her observance: it was driven both by her longing for her childhood home and the customs that had been so central to her mother's life, and by the feeling of unity it continued to give her with the broader Jewish community. Her friends were clearly baffled by her attempts to explain her adherence to this decidedly non-modern and non-intellectual practice. And in a humorous poke at their own lack of understanding, Feygenberg described how her assimilated girlfriend had an epiphany that Feygenberg's religious practice must mean that she is a Zionist, while Sergei expounded with firm conviction on the conclusion from his scholarly research that it is a requirement for Zionists to divorce their wives.

Feygenberg spent at least four and a half years in Saint Petersburg and was there until 1910 or so. She spent about a year in Switzerland in 1911–12, where she studied language and literature at the University of Lausanne and learned French, but she was unable to afford to stay on longer.[9] She then moved to Warsaw, which had a rich Yiddish literary scene, and became good friends with Sore Reyzen, the poet, writer, and sister of the author Avrom Reyzen and the lexicographer Zalman Reyzen, who would go on to compile an extensive reference work of biographies and bibliographies of Yiddish writers.[10]

Throughout this period, she continued writing. In addition to the six stories she had published during 1906–8, she published her somewhat revised version of *My Childhood Years* in book form in 1909, five stories in newspapers from 1909–11, a novella called *A Mother* in book form in 1911, an impressive twelve stories in 1912 alone, and another half dozen in 1913–14. In Warsaw, she also met the famous novelist Mordkhe Spektor, who became something of a mentor and a father figure to Feygenberg, who looked on him "as if he were an old relative, or one of my father's friends from my childhood in my small shtetl."[11] Spektor and his wife Berta welcomed her to their modest home on a daily basis, where he chastised her good-naturedly but repeatedly for not making some practical purpose out of her life and for her "pointless literary dreams, which would always, always remove her further from serious business"—by which he may have meant that she should write something more serious than stories, or as Judith Levin astutely pointed out in her thesis about

Feygenberg, he may have meant that the writer, now in her late twenties, should be thinking about getting married.[12]

In 1914, Feygenberg did just that. She fell in love with a pharmacist named Gronem (also called Gedaliahu) Shapira, a relative of her mother who was twenty-five years her senior and who used to visit them in her childhood home; married; and moved to the small shtetl of Yanovka outside Odesa. She gave birth to a son, Israel, in 1915.[13] For six years, she set down her pen and settled in to the life of a small-shtetl housewife and mother. This period closed the first chapter of her life as a writer. However, for Feygenberg, much of the work for which she would become most renowned would come in the future, and it would have the nature of a very practical purpose indeed: her journalism, including her pogrom documentation, her work as a correspondent from Mandatory Palestine, and her weekly column for over a decade for the Warsaw-based *Moment* newspaper. In the 1920s and 1930s, Feygenberg became one of the most widely read Yiddish writers in eastern Europe.

Rokhl Feygenberg's Mature Years as a Writer

The events that shook Feygenberg out of her life of domesticity were even more dramatic than those that had affected her childhood: the upheaval caused by the 1919 Ukrainian pogroms during the years of civil war that followed the 1917 Russian Revolution. Conservative minimum estimates are that 50,000 Jews were killed during these pogroms, and countless more raped and otherwise injured, in a shocking scale of brutality that was unprecedented in modern times.[14] Feygenberg told her mentor, Mordkhe Spektor, about her own harrowing escape in the fall of 1919:

> After the terrible summer of the Jewish massacres, when I hid with my child in my arms among the peasants from the nearby villages, I came at last to Odesa. I went right away to Spektor and told him my Ukrainian saga, how my nice, small-shtetl home with the acacias under the windows was destroyed, and how I traveled to the city under the fear of death. A kind Bulgarian peasant woman along the way gave me her holiday dress with its national colors and I put a cross around the neck of my little boy, since there were still Jewish corpses lying on the highway to Balta, and there were still placards hanging on the telephone poles from General Grigoriev that said that all Jewish boys should be killed, because when they grew up, they would all become communists.[15]

Spektor listened to her gravely, then urged her to join a small group of writers that were going out into the community to document the devastation the Jews had endured. Feygenberg did so, noting that some of the refugees bore witness to experiences that "made the blood in my veins run cold," and the writers began revising the material they had collected into the form of narratives. This was the start of the journalistic writing for which Rokhl Feygenberg would become most well-known. When in 1920 she went to her old friend, the renowned poet Khayim-Nakhman Bialik, and read him a draft of her new book *Under the Hammer* about her own experiences as well as testimonies of survivors she had collected in Odesa, Bialik told her she must start writing again: "This is your burden and you must bear it." While Feygenberg at first resisted Bialik's "prophecy," it would indeed become true, as she later reflected: "Since then, I have had no escape from my writing."[16] What had begun as a childhood urge to write had turned into a mission—Feygenberg had found the practical purpose of her life.

When she could not find a publisher for the Yiddish version of *Under the Hammer*, the book was published in Hebrew translation in 1923, and she published two more books of pogrom journalism: *On the Banks of the Dniester* in 1925, documenting the lives of refugees who had settled in the towns along the river, and *The Destruction of Dubova: The Chronicle of a Dead City* in 1926.[17] In addition to these books, she contributed many articles about the pogroms to newspapers in Kishinev, New York, and Warsaw. She also spent a year in Paris during 1926–27 participating in the defense of Sholem Schwartzbard in his murder trial after he assassinated Symon Petliura, the political leader who was deemed responsible for the Ukrainian pogroms. Schwartzbard, who had lost many members of his family in the blood-bath, was acquitted.

Feygenberg's husband Gronem Shapira and their son Israel immigrated to Mandatory Palestine circa 1921, probably at the same time she left Ukraine and moved across the border to Kishinev, Romania (modern Chişinău, Moldova), where she published accounts of the Ukrainian pogroms in articles for newspapers and in her books.[18] Her letters to him during their separation offer a rare look into her personal life as an adult.[19] "The fact that our child is not staying in one place is making me crazy," she writes in an early letter to him, and she arranges for her aunt Nekhama to go take care of the boy. "Until I come, she must take care of this little bird of mine. She must do it. I have no one besides her. . . . Dear God, give me strength to bear it!" In a postscript to little Izele, about seven years old at the time, she asks, "Do you like Palestine?" and asks him to draw her a picture of their hotel. When Gronem has a problem with a poorly translated document that attests to his being a pharmacist, Feygenberg is able to secure a copy of his diploma for him. "The sacred word 'pharmacist' will be written" on the new documents, she tells him wryly. Her husband also has an interest in beekeeping, but Feygenberg advises him that it would be better for him to arrange a job as a pharmacist before investing in beehives. The letters juxtapose the mundane with the serious. "Write me how often Izinke goes to school," she writes in the same letter as she tells Gronem how rattled she is about the tragic suicide of someone she knew called Frumke. "It seems that something terrible may have happened to her in Yanovka," she wrote, "I should have taken care of her. I'm completely broken down."

In 1924, Feygenberg joined her family in Mandatory Palestine, and late that year, she joined the staff of the prestigious Warsaw newspaper *Der moment* as a correspondent.[20] The eleven years during which she worked for *Der moment*, one of the preeminent daily papers published in eastern Europe, were the most prolific in her life, and she wrote hundreds of columns, stories, essays, and polemics during those years as well as several novels and plays; it was then that she became one of the most recognized Yiddish writers in Europe. In 1926, she returned to Europe for three and a half years, then went back to Palestine, and subsequently spent yet another year in Europe. During her years away from Palestine, she traveled extensively throughout Europe and especially Poland, receiving warm welcomes from her audiences whenever she gave readings. In 1933, she settled in Palestine permanently. Throughout her eleven years at *Der moment*, her weekly columns, published on Fridays, were immensely popular, and she built a large, loyal fanbase of readers who saved her columns to read aloud to their families.[21]

By the early 1930s, Feygenberg was undergoing a transformation in her own thinking, moving away

from Yiddish and toward Hebrew, a shift which she
made decisively in 1936 when she stopped writing for
Der moment. She reasoned that, to promote accul-
turation and to build a sense of Jewish nationalism
in their nascent home in Mandatory Palestine, immigrants should be encouraged to adopt their "new
native tongue" as quickly as possible, while those
who wanted to speak Yiddish should live in what had
now become the Soviet Union.[22] Dismissed by the Zionist literati, who felt it was important to promote
their ideology by translating works of Hebrew into
Yiddish, which at the time was much more widely
understood, she argued that it was instead vital for
classic works of Yiddish to be translated into Hebrew; she contended that this was culturally important as well as a pragmatic pedagogical approach to
encourage immigrants to learn their new language.
She translated her own books—with the exception of
My Childhood Years, as noted in the Introduction—
and in 1945 founded a publishing house at personal
expense to translate Yiddish works into Hebrew
using the normally omitted vowels, to make it easier for Hebrew learners to read; however, the venture
failed after publishing three books by I. J. Singer,
Dovid Bergelson, and Moshe Kulbak. During World
War II, the practice of translating Yiddish classics to
Hebrew did catch on more widely, as a way for Hebrew readers in Mandatory Palestine to connect to
their European coreligionists. In this way, translation
ended up transformed from a pedagogical tool for

immigrants to learn a new language into a task of cultural preservation.[23]

Rokhl Feygenberg, Writer

By 1936, when Feygenberg began writing primarily in Hebrew, she had published seven books in Yiddish: three novels (*A Mother*, 1911; *Strange Ways*, 1925; and *A Two-Year Marriage*, 1932), two of pogrom journalism (previously mentioned), and a polemic called *The World Wants Us To Be Jews* (1936) that argued against assimilation, as well as her premiere, the autobiographical bildungsroman *My Childhood Years*. But the overwhelming volume of her Yiddish output of over four hundred pieces was published in the ephemeral medium of the press. In her heyday in the 1920s and 1930s, when she was writing for *Der moment*, her weekly pieces were printed every Friday across the full width of the paper, with banner headlines and her name in large font. As the writer Rokhl Auerbach commented in a later appraisal, "There was not a Yiddish reader in Poland who didn't know her."[24]

But Feygenberg had also gained a reputation as a belligerent. When in 1926 she discovered that her editors at *Der moment* were removing material from her series from Palestine, *Builders of the New Ancient Land*, and adding material that she hadn't written, Feygenberg packed up and went back to Warsaw to confront them in person.[25] She ended up staying in Europe for three and a half years, winning the right to write her own truth, and continuing to attract a large, loyal readership, but doing some amount of lasting damage to her working relationship with those in the publishing world. "Rokhl Feygenberg is not only a fighter for rights and her truth but also for ordinary truth," her old friend Melech Ravitch commented in 1945, adding somewhat wistfully, "Whenever she appeared in Warsaw full of combativeness for her rights . . . it always resulted in some damage and a broken head from her forcefully belaboring her point. But such was her nature."[26] Back in Palestine, she never really regained her footing as a preeminently popular writer in her "new native tongue."

Feygenberg's commitment to tell her truth, complete with nuance, resulted in some uncomfortable stories. In her contribution to a 1929 volume of reminiscences of her mentor Mordkhe Spektor, published after his death, Feygenberg recalled the days of gathering eyewitness accounts from the survivors of the terrible Ukrainian pogroms of 1919. Back in the editorial office, she said, as the writers were shaping the testimonials into the form of narratives, one of her fellow writers read aloud a story about a Jewish Red Army soldier who, out of vengeance for his murdered father, had killed a gentile peasant woman together with her newborn infant. As Feygenberg related, Spektor became extremely agitated, crying, "No, it's a lie!" and ordered the writer to remove the description from the narrative. It seems that the description was indeed removed, but the terrible story was memorable enough for Feygenberg that she documented it in her reminiscence a decade later, despite the questionable light that it reflected on her beloved mentor.[27]

Feygenberg's "combative" nature was undoubtedly shaped both by her supremely difficult life experiences as well as by her simply being among the first women to write professionally in a Yiddish world that had no place for such a thing. *My Childhood Years* had been received positively, if somewhat paternalistically, as the sincere and straightforward writing of a "naive" young girl, and as she matured, her style remained similarly direct; she wrote from her own witnessed experience, framing her writing with the same kind of insightful observations that can already be seen in *My Childhood Years*. But writing her truth, which might have been welcomed from a young girl and inspired compassion for a young orphan, resulted in her being marked as contrarian as she matured, a kind of self-fulfilling label that is tinged with misogyny.

The independence of her thinking also frames her broader life as one of struggle and contradiction. As a girl in a small shtetl at a time when there were no schools for girls, she desperately wanted an education, and she fought to read literature in a place that had none. Despite coming from a family of intellectuals and Zionists, she had proletarian and socialist sympathies. As a young woman deliberately pursuing the manual occupation of sewing, she worked not in a sweatshop but in a "high-end" women's salon. Despite her dim view of the intelligentsia, after the age of twenty she never again worked with her hands. She was an intellectual, but she continued her religious practice. She was religious, but she wrote racy novels (by the standards of the time). She moved to Palestine, but she was not a Zionist. She was not a Zionist, but she strongly advocated for the creation of a national Jewish identity.[28] Despite her socialist sympathies, she disapproved of the socialist-influenced kibbutzim in Palestine because she thought children should live with their families rather than be raised in communal living quarters.[29] She was supremely family oriented in her writing, and her life was strongly shaped by the premature loss of her mother, but in pursuit of her work as a writer, she lived apart from her own young child for years at a time, on more than one occasion.

Feygenberg herself may have struggled with these contradictions; she certainly noted her status as a perpetual outsider. In old age, she complained bitterly about the fact that, despite the fact that she had never stopped writing, and despite the fact that her desk drawers were overflowing with unpublished manuscripts, and despite routinely being asked by her fans why she had "stopped writing," it was her publishers who refused to put forward her works.[30] When at the age of seventy she wrote an autobiographical piece for her archive at the Gnazim Institute in Tel Aviv, she signed the piece with her Hebrew-language moniker "Rakhel Imri," as she was known in Israel.[31]

But underneath, as if to compactly acknowledge the complexity of her life, she added, "Rokhl Feygenberg, in exile."

Rokhl Feygenberg continued to write stories, articles, and books, primarily in Hebrew and occasionally in Yiddish, until her death in Tel Aviv in 1972, and she left behind a trove of published works as well as unpublished manuscripts in Yiddish and in Hebrew. Whether or not the label of "fighter" is justified, it is clear that Feygenberg was fiercely independent, driven by personal conviction, and strenuously resistant of all labels aside from one: that of "writer."[32] As a pursuit she had begun as a child and continued until her death at the age of eighty-seven, it is a label that can be endorsed with gratitude to a remarkable woman for a distinguished body of work produced throughout her extraordinary life and times.

Acknowledgments

*Glossary and Explanation
of Terms*

Notes

Translator's Bibliography

Acknowledgments

In the way that one thing leads to another, I first found out about Rokhl Feygenberg via Ruth Murphy, who had published her translations of the exceptional short stories by the Yiddish writer Salomea Perl, *The Canvas and Other Stories*, in 2021. During an online discussion of *The Canvas*, Ruth referenced pivotal research by Nurit Orchan on early women writers in the Yiddish press in czarist Russia, which Nurit had summarized in an excellent article for the Jewish Women's Archive, "Women's Participation in Eastern European Yiddish Press." Nurit paid special tribute to Rokhl Feygenberg as one of the best of the early Yiddish women writers, and my curiosity was piqued. When I began reading Feygenberg's autobiographical *My Childhood Years*, it immediately resonated with my longtime fascination with the intersection of genealogy, history, and storytelling. I'm deeply grateful to both Ruth and Nurit for our subsequent correspondences about the project and especially to Ruth, who had already published the translation of a chapter of *My Childhood Years* on the website of the Yiddish Book Center when she generously gave me her blessing to take on the translation of the entire work.

I began learning Yiddish as a pandemic whim without realizing how beguiling it would become for me; I expected it to be enjoyable but had no idea how much the culture, religion, and history of its speakers was embedded in the language. For this realization, I'm especially grateful to Dovid Braun, Anna Fishman Gonshor, Joshua Price, and my many other teachers and fellow students at YIVO, especially during my four summer intensives at YIVO's Uriel Weinreich Program in Yiddish Language, Literature and Culture. Dovid, Anna, and Josh opened my eyes to the richness of the language and literature; their passion sparked my own and their encouragement has been priceless.

It was an honor to be a 2023 Translation Fellow at the Yiddish Book Center, whose support made this work possible. An excerpt of this translation was published on the Yiddish Book Center website. Thanks very much to Madeleine Cohen, Margaret Frothingham, and the staff at the Yiddish Book Center for their help throughout and beyond my fellowship year, to our terrific workshop leaders, and to my fellow fellows for their friendship, camaraderie, and helpful discussions along the way. I'm deeply grateful to my fellowship mentor, Ellen Cassedy, who patiently read every word, gave me detailed critical feedback, and taught me to move my translation forward out of "Yiddishland" and into "Englishland." I'm also grateful to translator and workshop leader Bill Johnston for his advice and encouragement.

Hila Tzur and the staff at the Gnazim Institute in Tel Aviv were generous in helping me access Rokhl Feygenberg's archive, and I'm grateful to Miriam Tisch for her many trips to Gnazim on my behalf. I thank archivist Ruby

Landau-Pincus at YIVO for sending me copies of several pages of the original manuscript of *Di kinder-yohren* that had been missing from the microfilm copies.

I have benefited from many wonderful resources while working on this translation and researching its historical context. Sheva Zucker's very helpful article on the Jewish Women's Archive, "Rokhl Faygnberg (Imri)," grounded my first research into Feygenberg's life. Judith Levin's Hebrew-language thesis, "From Lyuban, Lithuania, to Tel-Aviv: Milestones in Rochl Feigenberg's Literary Work, 1885–1933," was an invaluable resource; her extensive bibliography of representative writings from Feygenberg's career as a journalist was especially helpful, and I'm very grateful to Judith for sending me her thesis. I thank Elissa Bemporad for kindly sharing an advance copy of her introduction to the new translation of Feygenberg's pogrom account, *The Destruction of Dubova: Chronicle of a Dead City*. Annie Cohen's website, "Pulling at Threads," was an excellent reference on women's religious customs and roles in Ashkenazi Jewish culture. Marek Tuszewicki's *A Frog Under the Tongue: Jewish Folk Medicine in Eastern Europe* helped me understand the nuances of many different kinds of trained and untrained healers. I owe tremendous debt to the collective knowledge of the "Yidforsh" Yiddish Research group on Facebook, whose experts were able to guide me through sticky passages and obscure references.

I am grateful to Heather Stauffer and Syracuse University Press for guiding this work to publication. Heather's suggestions, mildly stated but keen and to the point, invariably made the book better. I thank Jessica Kirzane and Rachel Mines, whose thoughtful and careful critical reviews helped me make several improvements to the text.

The unattributed, undated map of Feygenberg's birth shtetl of Lyuban that appears in the Introduction was originally published with Hebrew and Yiddish labels in the *Slutsk and Vicinity Memorial Book*, and I thank Patrick Remer and Zinnia Heinzmann for producing the nice version of the map with English labels. I'm very grateful to Lance Ackerfeld and the JewishGen Yizkor Book Project for their permission to use Jerrold Landau's translation of Feygenberg's "Lyubanites of My Mother's Family" from the Slutsk book in writing the new epilogue of *The Winding Road*. More broadly, I'm grateful to JewishGen for their invaluable work collecting a bibliography of over one thousand memorial books of former communities in eastern Europe and for their ongoing work translating these books into English.

I thank Aisha Ginwalla, Benjamin Lerman, and Bikram Phookun for reading the draft at various stages and offering very helpful feedback and suggestions along with their encouragement, and to John, Benjamin, and Joseph Lugten and my entire family for their constant love and support while I've been deep in Yiddishland.

I'm grateful to Rokhl Feygenberg's granddaughter, Daphna Levy, for her helpful correspondence about her grandmother and for sending me the picture of Feygenberg that appears in the frontispiece, and to Feygenberg's great-granddaughter, Sharon Marcus, for a lovely coffee together. Their very presence is a reminder of *di goldene keyt*, the "golden chain" of connection from generation to generation, and helped bring me closer to Feygenberg herself.

My primary debt is to Rokhl Feygenberg for writing this remarkable book. I've felt her looking over my shoulder with a slight frown on her face, and I hope she would think I've done justice to her work. This translation is dedicated to the memory of the young Rokhl Feygenberg and the writer she became.

Glossary and Explanation of Terms

afikomen: a piece of matzo set aside to be eaten at the end of the Passover seder.

challah: a braided egg bread eaten by Jews on Sabbath and holidays.

Chanukah: an eight-day holiday commemorating the re-dedication of the Second Temple of Jerusalem around 164 BCE, usually in late fall or early winter.

cheder: a Jewish elementary school where boys were traditionally taught Hebrew and Torah.

chuppah: a canopy for Jewish weddings.

Elijah: Hebrew prophet who lived in the ninth century BCE. During the Passover seder, a cup of wine is poured for Elijah as a symbol of future redemption, and the door of the house is opened to invite Elijah in.

erev: the eve before a holiday or Shabbes; Jewish holidays and Shabbes begin at sunset.

gabbai: manager of a synagogue.

Gemara: part of the Talmud consisting of rabbinical analysis and commentary by sages.

golem: a soulless, humanlike creature made of clay and artificially brought to life; part of Jewish folklore.

Haggadah: a narrative of the biblical exodus of the Jews from Egypt read during a Passover seder.

Hasid: a member of a Jewish movement characterized by spiritual revivalism.

havdalah: a ritual marking the close of Shabbes and the beginning of the new week.

kabbalah: a Jewish mystical tradition.

kaddish: the mourner's prayer recited in memory of the dead.

kapores: a ritual of atonement for erev Yom Kippur, where a live chicken or rooster was swung over a person's head, then slaughtered in accordance with religious law and eaten.

kapote: a long coat or kaftan, formerly worn by male Jews in eastern Europe.

kiddush: blessing spoken over a ceremonial cup of wine to sanctify Shabbes or a holiday.

kittel: a man's white robe of cotton or linen, worn especially on solemn holidays and sometimes as a burial shroud.

klasikers: classical authors, often used to refer to the trio of Yiddish authors of Sholem Aleichem (pen name of Shalom Rabinowitz), Yitskhok Leybush Peretz, and Mendele Mokher Sforim (pen name of Sholem Yankev Abramovitch).

Korakh: a Biblical Jew who was punished for leading a rebellion against Moses.

kosher meat tax: a burdensome tax on the slaughter of cattle and fowl and on the sale of meat, imposed on Jews by the Russian government.

maggid: an itinerant Jewish preacher, a teller of religious stories rather than a rabbi.

Maskil: a follower of the Jewish Enlightenment movement called the Haskalah, an intellectual rationalist movement that encouraged secular education as well as religious studies.

melamed (pl. melamdim): a religious teacher or tutor of children.

meshuga: crazy, insane; eccentric.

minyan: the quorum of ten adult men required for public communal worship.

mitzvah: a religious obligation that must be performed to fulfill a commandment from God; a good deed.

mizrach: a sacred picture hung on the eastern wall of a house, to indicate the direction of Jerusalem, which Jews face in prayer.

Moyshe Rabenu: Moses our Teacher, the prophet Moses.

opshprekher, opshprekherin: a kind of (male, female) folk healer who employs a mixture of incantations, movements, charms, and herbal and natural remedies.

panienke (Polish): young lady.

Passover: a major Jewish holiday that commemorates the biblical exodus of the Jews from Egypt, usually in early spring.

Pesach: Passover.

peyes: sidelocks, worn by some observant Jewish men. The practice was banned in Russia by Tsar Nicholas I in 1845.

Reb: honorific title, similar to "Mr."

rebbe: a Hasidic rabbi.

rebbetzin: the wife of a rabbi.

Romani: a member of a traditionally itinerant people who have lived in Europe for centuries.

Rosh Hashanah: the Jewish New Year, usually in late summer or early fall. Rosh Hashanah and Yom Kippur comprise the High Holy Days.

seder: a ceremonial dinner held at home during the first night of Passover.

selichos: penitential prayers, said especially in the period leading up to Rosh Hashanah and Yom Kippur.

Shabbes: the Jewish Sabbath, which begins on Friday evening.

shammes: a caretaker or sexton in a synagogue.

Shavuos: a holiday that celebrates God's giving of the Torah to the Jews, usually in late spring.

Shema or *Shema Yisroel*: the centerpiece of Jewish prayer, traditionally recited daily in the morning and the evening as a religious commandment.

Shevat Musar: an ethical treatise composed by Eliyahu HaKohen of Smyrna in 1712, divided into fifty-two chapters, one for every week of the year.

sheytl: a wig worn by some observant married Jewish women as a sign of modesty.

shiva: the traditional seven-day period of mourning for the death of a family member.

shlimazel: an unlucky or incompetent person.

shofar: a ram's horn blown in ritualistic blasts during Rosh Hashanah and Yom Kippur services.

shoykhet: a ritual slaughterer of animals used for food.

shtetl: a small, predominantly Jewish market town.

shul: a synagogue.

siddur: a Jewish prayer book with a collection of essential prayers for the entire year.

Simchas Torah: the holiday celebration of the completion of the annual cycle of public Torah readings and the beginning of the new cycle.

sukkah: a temporary, symbolic shelter with a roof of branches and leaves that is erected and used for meals and other purposes during the week of Sukkos.

Sukkos: a week-long, Jewish fall harvest festival.

Talmud: the authoritative text of Rabbinic Judaism, containing religious law, theology, philosophy, folklore, commentary, and other topics.

Tanakh: the Jewish scriptures, which includes the Torah, the prophets, and collected writings.

tchotchke: a knick-knack or toy.

tkhine: a Yiddish-language prayer or devotional, usually written for women.

Torah: the Law, also called the Pentateuch, or the first five books of the Jewish scriptures.

tsaddik (**pl.** *tsaddikim*): a righteous or saintly man.

Tzedakah tatzil mimavet (**Hebrew**): "Charity saves from death," a phrase from the book of Proverbs that serves as a reminder of the importance of charitable giving.

viddui: the confession of sin, recited as part of the liturgy at Yom Kippur or privately before death.

Volhynia: a historic geographic region located in what is today northwest Ukraine, extending somewhat past the borders of modern Poland and Belarus.

White Russia: Belarus.

yeshiva: an advanced school for Talmudic studies.

yetzer hara: an innate inclination toward evil.

yetzer toyv: an innate inclination toward good.

Yom Kippur: the Day of Atonement, the holiest of Jewish holidays, which is organized around atonement and repentance and occurs ten days after the Jewish New Year, Rosh Hashanah.

zogerin: a female prayer leader, usually in a synagogue but sometimes in a cemetery or as a professional mourner.

Zohar: the foundational work of Jewish mysticism, or kabbalah.

Notes

Translator's Introduction

1. See Ginzburg, "Well-Known Writer," for the following details of Ginzburg's recollection.

2. Novershtern, "About This Newspaper."

3. "Russian Railroad Maps 1877–1912," https://www .germansfromrussiasettlementlocations.org/2021/03/russian -railroad-maps-1877-1912.html (accessed May 4, 2025).

4. Even-Shoshan, "Province of Minsk."

5. Lipshitz, "Memories of Hlusk."

6. Even-Shoshan, "Province of Minsk."

7. Feigenberg, "My Town."

8. Holtzman, "Epstein, Zalman."

9. The names of the daughters and the following description are from Feygenberg, "Three Generations."

10. Lipshitz, "Memories of Hlusk."

11. Feigenberg-Omry, "Lyubanites."

12. Feygenberg, "Details from My History."

13. Feygenberg, "Details from My History."

14. In 1888, Sholem Aleichem had famously issued a 100-page diatribe against Shomer, whose works at the time were outselling the young Sholem Aleichem's by a factor of thirty. Quint, "Yiddish Literature for the Masses," 81. It is notable that a writer of Feygenberg's stature came of age not under the influence of the *klasikers* of Yiddish literature but under the influence

of this crasser genre, a point that underscores the broad creative influences on early women Yiddish writers.

15. Reyzen, "Feygenberg, Rokhl," 1926.

16. "Russian Railroad Maps 1877–1912."

17. The fictionalized name is a reference to the fifth Duke de Richelieu, who became the first governor of Odesa in 1803; a statue of the duke stands at the top of the famous Potemkin Stairs, which in Feygenberg's time was called the "Richelieu Steps."

18. Zipperstein, "Odessa."

19. Feygenberg, "Details from My History."

20. See Feygenberg, "Three Generations," for the following account of how she came to write *My Childhood Years*.

21. Ginzburg, "Well-Known Writer."

22. Feygenberg, "Three Generations."

23. Holtzman, "Epstein, Zalman."

24. Tidhar, "Dr. Yitzhak Epstein."

25. Feygenberg, "Details from My History."

26. Anecdote from Feygenberg, "Three Generations."

27. These kinds of childhood reminiscences were not unusual in Russian spheres, having been popularized by the likes of Tolstoy. Clyman and Vowles, *Russia Through Women's Eyes*.

Translation Notes

1. Feigenberg-Omry, "Lyubanites."

2. Levin, "From Lyuban to Tel-Aviv."

Translator's Afterword

1. Prilutski, "Poetic Tribute."

2. Ginzburg, "Well-Known Writer."

3. Zipperstein, "Odessa."

4. Nathans, "Saint Petersburg."

5. Enrollment jumped from 6,800 in 1906 to 17,000 in 1908. Dudgeon, "Women Students in Imperial Russia," 9.

6. Feygenberg, "Details from My History"; Feygenberg, "Three Generations."

7. Dudgeon, "Women Students in Imperial Russia," 17.

8. Feygenberg, "Moderne fanatiker."

9. Reyzen, "Feygenberg, Rokhl," 1914; Levin, "From Lyuban to Tel-Aviv," 10.

10. In an undated letter from Sore Reyzen to Feygenberg, probably from the mid-1920s, Reyzen writes, "Zalman sends his greetings and thanks you for your autobiography." It seems likely that most or all of the personal information on Feygenberg in Zalman Reyzen's classic *Leksikon* was provided by Feygenberg herself. Levin, "From Lyuban to Tel-Aviv," 9.

11. Feygenberg, "Spektor der privat-mentsh."

12. Levin, "From Lyuban to Tel-Aviv," 18.

13. Feygenberg addressed her husband as "Gronem" in personal correspondence, but their granddaughter referred to him as "Gedaliahu." Details from Feygenberg's archive, Gnazim Institute; personal correspondence from Daphna Levy (August 29, 2023, and December 10, 2024); Reyzen, "Feygenberg, Rokhl," 1926; and Ravitch, "Rokhl Feygenberg."

14. Kleir, "Pogroms."

15. Feygenberg, "Spektor der privat-mentsh."

16. Feygenberg, "Details from My History."

17. Levin, "From Lyuban to Tel-Aviv," 90–91.

18. Feygenberg's 1921 move to Kishinev is referenced in Reyzen, "Feygenberg, Rokhl," 1926.

19. The fact and timing of Gronem Shapira's move to Mandatory Palestine with their young son may be inferred from letters Feygenberg wrote to Gronem that are held in Feygenberg's archive at the Gnazim Institute. This correspondence includes five undated letters and a postcard with a blurred date (probably from 1921) written from Feygenberg to her husband. Four of the items were written from Kishinev, and the postcard is addressed to her husband in Tel Aviv; from the content of the

correspondence, it is clear that he and their son are living in Palestine. In one letter, she reports that "the writing of Dubova is almost done," and it's known that she wrote the first version of her book about the 1919 Dubova pogroms between late 1921 and early 1922 (see Elissa Bemporad's Introduction to Faygnberg, *The Destruction of Dubova*). The fifth letter was written from Merhavia, a kibbutz in Palestine, so it must date from after Feygenberg moved to Palestine in 1924. The existence of Feygenberg's letters to her husband corrects the previously published notion that Gronem Shapira died circa 1919.

20. Feygenberg, "Details from My History."

21. Feygenberg, "Details from My History."

22. Feygenberg, "Details from My History."

23. Brenner, "Translating Yiddish."

24. Auerbach, "Rokhl Feygenberg," 212.

25. Feygenberg, "Vegn zikh aleyn."

26. Ravitch, "Rokhl Feygenberg."

27. Feygenberg, "Spektor der privat-mentsh."

28. Feygenberg, *Di velt vil mir zoln zayn yidn*.

29. Levin, "From Lyuban to Tel-Aviv," 189.

30. Feygenberg, "Details from My History," and Feygenberg, "Vegn zikh aleyn."

31. Feygenberg, "Details from My History."

32. Feygenberg, "Moderne fanatiker."

Translator's Bibliography

Auerbach, Rokhl. "Rokhl Feygenberg." In *Di goldene keyt*, no. 17 (1953): 212–15.

Brenner, Naomi. "Bound Up in the Bond of Hebrew Literature: Translating Yiddish in the 1940s," in *Lingering Bilingualism: Modern Hebrew and Yiddish Literatures in Contact*. Syracuse Univ. Press, 2016.

Clyman, Toby W., and Judith Vowles, eds. *Russia Through Women's Eyes: Autobiographies from Tsarist Russia*. Yale Univ. Press, 1996.

Cohen, Annabel Gottfried. "Pulling at Threads." Accessed February 1, 2025. https://pullingatthreads.com.

Dudgeon, Ruth A. "The Forgotten Minority: Women Students in Imperial Russia, 1872–1917." *Russian History* 9, no. 1 (1982): 1–26. http://www.jstor.org/stable/24652820.

Even-Shoshan, Shlomo. "Province of Minsk." In *Minsk, Jewish Mother City: A Memorial Anthology*, edited by David Kohen and Shlomo Even-Shoshan. Translated by Jerrold Landau. Assoc. of Olim from Minsk and Its Surroundings in Israel, 1975–85. http://www.jewishgen.org/yizkor/minsk/minsk.html.

Faygenberg, Rokhl. *Strange Ways.* Translated by Robert and Golda Werman. Gefen Publishing House, 2007.

Faygnberg, Rokhl. *The Destruction of Dubova: Chronicle of a Dead City.* Translated by Cynthia Madansky. Bloomsbury, 2025.

Feigenberg, Rachel. "My Town That Is No More." In *Slutsk and Vicinity Memorial Book,* edited by Nahum Chinitz and Shimshon Nachmani. Translated by Jerrold Landau. Yizkor-Book Committee, 1962. http://www.jewishgen.org/Yizkor/slutsk/slutsk.html.

Feigenberg-Omry, Rachel. "Lyubanites of My Mother's Family." In *Slutsk and Vicinity Memorial Book*, edited by Nahum Chinitz and Shimshon Nachmani. Translated by Jerrold Landau. Yizkor-Book Committee, 1962. http://www.jewishgen.org/Yizkor/slutsk/slutsk.html.

Feygenberg, Rokhl. *Di velt vil mir zoln zayn yidn* [*The World Wants Us To Be Jews*]. Farn folk, 1936.

Feygenberg, Rokhl. "Moderne fanatiker" [Modern Fanatics]. *Der moment*, February 17, 1928.

Feygenberg, Rokhl. "My First Readers." In *Beautiful As the Moon, Radiant As the Stars*, edited by Sandra Bark. Translated by Sheva Zucker. Grand Central Publishing, 2007.

Feygenberg, Rokhl. Personal correspondence to her husband Gronem Shapira. Gnazim Institute, Rokhl Feygenberg Archives (602), Reference 308654, 1921 and undated.

Feygenberg, Rokhl. "Questionnaire" [in Hebrew]. Gnazim Institute, Rokhl Feygenberg Archives (602), Reference 16543, undated.

Feygenberg, Rokhl. "Some Details from My History" [in Hebrew]. Gnazim Institute, Rokhl Feygenberg Archives (602), Reference 3873/1, 1955.

Feygenberg, Rokhl. "Spektor der privat-mentsh" [Spektor the Private Man]. In *Spektor-bukh*, compiled by David Kassel. Ahisefer, 1929.

Feygenberg, Rokhl. "Summary Chapters on the Lives of Three Generations of the Family" [in Hebrew]. Gnazim Institute, Rokhl Feygenberg Archives (602), Reference 33670, undated.

Feygenberg, Rokhl. "Vegn zikh aleyn" [About Myself]. *Heymish* 5, no. 45–46 (1960): 23–24; *Heymish* 5, no. 47 (1960): 10; *Heymish* 5, no. 50–52 (1960): 28–29; *Heymish* 5, no. 53–54 (1960): 8–9; *Heymish* 5, no. 55–56 (1960): 14; *Heymish* 5, no. 57–58 (1960): 18; *Heymish* 5, no. 59–60 (1960): 14; *Heymish* 6, no. 61–62 (1960): 11–12.

Ginzburg, Shaul. "A bevuste yidishe shrayberin vos hot itst aroysgegebn a hebreyish bukh" [A Well-Known Yiddish Writer Who Has Now Published a Hebrew Book]. *Forverts*, August 25, 1940.

Holtzman, Avner. 2010. "Epstein, Zalman." YIVO Encyclopedia of Jews in Eastern Europe, https://encyclopedia.yivo.org/article/675 (accessed May 4, 2025).

Klier, John. "Pogroms." YIVO Encyclopedia of Jews in Eastern Europe. https://encyclopedia.yivo.org/article/260 (accessed May 10, 2025).

Levin, Judith. "From Lyuban, Lithuania, to Tel-Aviv: Milestones in Rokhl Feygenberg's Literary Work, 1885–1933" [in Hebrew]. PhD diss., Bar-Ilan University, 2022.

Lipshitz, Yaakov. "Memories of Hlusk." In *Memorial Book of the Community of Bobruisk and Its Surroundings,* edited by Y. Slutski, Former Residents of Bobruisk in Israel and the USA. Translated by Sol Krongelb. Former Residents of Bobruisk in Israel and the USA, 1967. http://www.jewishgen.org/yizkor/bobruisk/bysktoc1.html.

Nathans, Benjamin. 2010. "Saint Petersburg." YIVO Encyclopedia of Jews in Eastern Europe. https://encyclopedia.yivo.org/article/329 (accessed February 20, 2025).

Novershtern, Avraham. "About This Newspaper: *Der fraynd.* Description." The National Library of Israel, https://www.nli.org.il/en/newspapers/dfr (accessed May 3, 2025).

Orchan, Nurit. "Yiddish: Women's Participation in Eastern European Yiddish Press (1862–1903)." Shalvi/Hyman Encyclopedia of Jewish Women. June 23, 2021. Jewish Women's Archive, https://jwa.org/encyclopedia/article/yiddish-womens-participation-in-eastern-european-yiddish-press-1862-1903 (accessed January 31, 2025).

Perl, Salomea. *The Canvas and Other Stories.* Translated by Ruth Murphy. Ben Yehuda Press, 2021.

Prilutski, N. "A yidishe kinder-poeme" [A Poetic Tribute to a Jewish Childhood]. *Leben un Visenshaft*, February 1, 1910.

Quint, Alyssa. "'Yiddish Literature for the Masses'? A Reconsideration of Who Read What in Jewish Eastern Europe." *AJS Review* 29, no. 1 (2005): 61–89. http://www.jstor.org/stable/4131809.

Ravitch, Melech. "Rokhl Feygenberg." *Mayn Leksikon*, vol. 3. Aroysgegebn fun a komitet, 1945.

Reyzen, Zalman. "Feygenberg, Rokhl." *Leksikon fun der yudisher literatur un prese*. Tsentral, 1914.

Reyzen, Zalman. "Feygenberg, Rokhl." *Leksikon fun der yudisher literatur, prese un filologye*, vol. 3. B. Kletskin, 1926.

Tidhar, D. "Dr. Yitzhak Epstein." *Entsiklopedyah le-halutse ha-yishuv u-vonav* (vol. 2, p. 822), 1947, https://www-tidhar-tourolib-org.translate.goog/tidhar/view/2/822 (accessed May 9, 2025).

Tuszewicki, Marek. *A Frog Under the Tongue: Jewish Folk Medicine in Eastern Europe*. Translated by Jessica Taylor-Kucia. The Littman Library of Jewish Civilization, 2021.

Zipperstein, Steven J. 2010. "Odessa." YIVO Encyclopedia of Jews in Eastern Europe, https://encyclopedia.yivo.org/article/897 (accessed May 9, 2025).

Zucker, Sheva. "Rokhl Faygnberg (Imri)." Shalvi/Hyman Encyclopedia of Jewish Women. February 27, 2009. Jewish Women's Archive, https://jwa.org/encyclopedia/article/faygnberg-imri-rokhl (accessed January 31, 2025).

Rokhl Feygenberg (1885–1972) was one of the earliest professional women authors published in Yiddish and became one of the most widely recognized Yiddish writers in eastern Europe in the 1920s and 1930s. Born in the small shtetl of Lyuban in White Russia (today's Belarus), her father died when she was about four, and her mother's serious illness that began when Feygenberg was twelve put an end to her formal education for many years, though she continued writing and storytelling. Following the early success of her debut, *My Childhood Years*, written while she was still a teenager, Feygenberg went on to publish stories, novels, plays, and essays, and she became a pogrom journalist after she herself survived a pogrom in Ukraine with her young son in 1919. She was a prolific literary prose writer and published hundreds of pieces as a correspondent for *Der moment* newspaper in Warsaw in the 1920s and 1930s. Feygenberg immigrated to Mandatory Palestine in 1924, returned to live again for several years in Europe, and settled permanently in Tel Aviv in 1933.

Translator Tamara T. Helfer is a former research astronomer, science educator, and program developer with broad interests in the intersection of history, genealogy, and storytelling. She was a 2023 Yiddish Book Center Translation Fellow. Her translation of *The Winding Road: My Childhood Years* by Rokhl Feygenberg was made possible with support from the Yiddish Book Center.